THE UNSTOPPABLES
TEAM ONE

MERRIED

AN UNSTOPPABLE CHRISTMAS

USA TODAY BESTSELLING AUTHOR

HEATHER SLADE

merry, *adj*

/ˈmer-ē/

full of gaiety or high spirits;
 mirthful

MORE FROM AUTHOR HEATHER SLADE

BUTLER RANCH
Kade's Worth
Brodie's Promise
Maddox's Truce
Naughton's Secret
Mercer's Vow
Kade's Return
Butler Ranch Christmas

WICKED WINEMAKERS
FIRST LABEL
Brix's Bid
Ridge's Release
Press' Passion
Zin's Sins
Tryst's Temptation

WICKED WINEMAKERS
SECOND LABEL
Beau's Beloved
Coming Soon:
Cru's Crush
Bones' Bliss
Snapper's Seduction
Kick's Kiss

ROARING FORK RANCH
Coming Soon:
Roaring Fork Wrangler
Roaring Fork Roughstock
Roaring Fork Rockstar
Roaring Fork Rooker
Roaring Fork Bridger

THE ROYAL AGENTS
OF MI6
Make Me Shiver
Drive Me Wilder
Feel My Pinch
Chase My Shadow
Find My Angel

K19 SECURITY
SOLUTIONS TEAM ONE
Razor's Edge
Gunner's Redemption
Mistletoe's Magic
Mantis' Desire
Dutch's Salvation

K19 SECURITY
SOLUTIONS TEAM TWO
Striker's Choice
Monk's Fire
Halo's Oath
Tackle's Honor
Onyx's Awakening

K19 SHADOW OPERATIONS
TEAM ONE
Code Name: Ranger
Code Name: Diesel
Code Name: Wasp
Code Name: Cowboy
Code Name: Mayhem

K19 ALLIED INTELLIGENCE
TEAM ONE
Code Name: Ares
Code Name: Cayman
Code Name: Poseidon
Code Name: Zeppelin
Code Name: Magnet

K19 ALLIED INTELLIGENCE
TEAM TWO
Coming Soon:
Code Name: Puck
Code Name: Michelangelo
Code Name: Typhon
Code Name: Hornet
Code Name: Reaper

PROTECTORS
UNDERCOVER
Undercover Agent
Undercover Emissary
Coming Soon:
Undercover Savior
Undercover Infidel
Undercover Assassin

THE INVINCIBLES
TEAM ONE
Decked
Edged
Grinded
Riled
Smoked

THE INVINCIBLES
TEAM TWO
Bucked
Irished
Sainted
Hammered
Ripped

THE UNSTOPPABLES
TEAM ONE
Furied
Merried

COWBOYS OF
CRESTED BUTTE
A Cowboy Falls
A Cowboy's Dance
A Cowboy's Kiss
A Cowboy Stays
A Cowboy Wins

Table of Contents

Chapter 1 1
Chapter 2 15
Chapter 3 30
Chapter 4 42
Chapter 5 55
Chapter 6 64
Chapter 7 75
Chapter 8 86
Chapter 9 97
Chapter 10 113
Chapter 11 122
Chapter 12 136
Chapter 13 144
Chapter 14 154
Epilogue 171
About the Author 175

1

Casper

"C'mon, Rile. You know I don't do shit like this."

"When I said 'everyone,' Casper, I meant *everyone.* That includes you. And here is what I know, my friend. You haven't celebrated Christmas since Beau died."

He was right, and I wasn't about to start now. Four years ago, on the second day of December, I received the visit every family member who has someone serving in the armed forces, an intelligence agency, or other types of law enforcement dreads.

While the CIA agents hadn't shown up at my house, when the man in charge of the mission I'd been assigned to called me into his office and two others I didn't recognize were already there, I knew. Beau had been killed in the line of duty.

I immediately asked to be recused from the mission and returned to the home Beau and I had shared in Florida since before we were married. Every year since, I'd managed to avoid Christmas parties, Christmas cards, Christmas everything.

"You're asking too much of me, Rile. If my refusal to attend means the Invincibles don't want me on their team anymore, I'll understand."

"There's more at stake, Calla. A new team has formed. It's headed by Fury Storm and Vex Dunning. At a meeting last week, the two gave us a list of those they'd like to extend partnerships to. Your name appeared first."

"Tell them to send me a proposal, and I'll look it over, but I'm not coming to a Christmas celebration to talk business or for any other reason. Nothing is going to make me change my mind."

"I'm sorry to hear you say those words. I pray something, or someone, will convince you to reconsider."

After ending the call, I went out to the backyard and sat on a chaise next to the swimming pool. While it rarely got above eighty in December on Di Lido Isle near Miami Beach, today was one of the rare times it got to almost ninety.

Our house, which we'd inherited from Beau's parents, was too big just for me, but I'd never leave it. The pool was one of the first things we'd replaced once we were able to afford to. After that, we remodeled the kitchen and transformed it into something sleek and modern. Then the bedrooms and bathrooms.

After Beau died, I'd briefly considered selling the place, but quickly changed my mind. While our time living here together had been too short, the memories we made were the best of my life.

I closed my eyes and raised my face to the warmth of the sun, remembering the last time we were here. Four years ago. Thanksgiving. We'd made a feast big enough to serve a dozen people for just the two of us because, as far as Beau was concerned, there was nothing better than Thanksgiving leftovers.

It was warm that week too, not that normal temperatures would've stopped us from swimming in the pool, lying in the sun, or making love on the outdoor bed.

"Dammit," I muttered when my cell rang. If it was Rile again, I'd let it go to voicemail. Instead, it was someone else I wasn't sure I wanted to talk to—Spider.

I let it ring one shy of it going to voicemail before hitting the accept button. "Hi," I answered.

"Casper. How's it goin'?"

I smiled, shook my head, and looked up at the sky. "Good, Spider. How are you?"

"I'm in your neighborhood. Thought I'd see if you wanted to meet for dinner."

I bolted upright. My neighborhood? I lived on a guarded-gate private island. "Where exactly?"

"Actually, not quite your neighborhood. I'm at my parents' place in Palm Beach."

I rested against the chaise, breathed a sigh of relief, and laughed. "Yeah, not quite, given you're at least two hours from here."

"The invitation still stands."

Spider was a nice enough guy. We'd gotten to know each other while working a serial killer investigation in the Adirondack State Park. I had no doubt those we worked with believed what developed between us was more than friendship. However, I didn't care what they thought. I never paid attention to anyone's opinions about me. Especially after Beau died.

"I don't think that's a good idea," I said, jarring myself back to Spider's call.

"There's something I want to run by you."

"What?"

"It's better if I tell you in person."

"What's the short version?"

"There isn't a short version. Come on, just have dinner with me. It's something that will benefit both of us."

I sighed. "When?

"Tonight."

I didn't have much food in the house, so I might as well let the man buy me dinner. "Where?"

"I'll pick you up."

This house was my sanctuary. The place where I came to get away from the rest of the world. I never invited anyone here. "The island is gated. It'll be easier if I meet you somewhere."

"I'll pick you up at seven. Wear something dressy."

"I don't do dressy."

"C'mon, Casper. Play along. If you don't have anything in your closet you would define as dressy, you have three hours to go out and get something."

Play along? What the hell did that mean? And *three hours*? Did he know nothing about Miami Beach traffic? Or women?

"See you at seven."

"Wait. No." Three chimes indicated the call had ended. Whether he'd heard me respond or not didn't matter. Spider would show up here anyway.

When the sun went behind a cloud, I made my way to look for something to wear. I was here so infrequently I couldn't remember what was in my closet.

"Slinky black dress, another slinky black dress. Those won't work. Way too sexy," I said out loud as I thumbed through the hangers. The next one was a maxi dress with long sleeves and a high collar. Since it was also black, it could qualify as "dressy." At least dressy enough.

I rummaged through my shoes, finding a pair of heels all the way in the corner. I hadn't worn heels since Beau died, mainly because I never did anything other than work and my job didn't call for stilettos. The other reason I didn't was my height. At five feet eleven, an extra two inches meant I was taller than most men. How did I know? I'd looked it up once. Only fourteen percent of men were six feet or over.

Beau had been six-three. While I didn't know exactly how tall Spider was, he was close to my husband's height. Maybe a little taller. Not that it mattered in this instance. It wasn't like this was a date. Spider said he had something he wanted to run by me and that it would benefit us both. It had to be work related.

At seven on the dot, the house phone rang. Given no one had the number besides the gatehouse, I knew they were calling to announce Spider's arrival. I answered and told them to let him in.

I still hadn't decided how to handle him showing up here but was leaning toward waiting outside so I didn't have to invite him in. I grabbed my clutch and rushed to the door, reaching it at the same time I heard a knock.

"Hi," I said, stunned when he stepped forward to kiss my cheek. "Um, do you want to come in?" Wait, hadn't I just decided not to invite him inside?

He looked at his watch. "We have to leave now if we're going to make our reservation."

"Excuse me."

He took a step back so I could close the door.

After I had, he led me to a red vintage Alfa Romeo Spider. I grinned. "Apropos."

His cheeks turned almost the same color as the car, and he rolled his eyes before opening the passenger door. "My dad's idea of the perfect sixteenth birthday present."

"It suits you."

He chuckled. "Yeah? I always feel like Magilla Gorilla when I drive it with the top down."

"Magilla Gorilla?"

"A cartoon from before you and I were born. My grandfather showed me a photo of the character driving a convertible and told me I looked just like it. After that, I couldn't get the image out of my head."

He shut my door and walked around to the other side of the car.

"Where are we going?" I asked when he got in and started the engine.

"It's a surprise."

"I don't like surprises, Spider."

He backed out of the driveway and drove in the direction of the gate. "Trust me."

Trust was an issue for me. The only man—only person besides my parents—I'd truly ever put my unfailing faith in was Beau. After he was killed, from all accounts by friendly fire, any belief I'd had in anyone protecting me, putting my best interest ahead of theirs, ended.

I suppose I had a modicum of confidence in the leaders of the two private security and intelligence firms I contracted for, but the idea that I was expendable—like my husband had been—never left the back of my mind.

"Raspoutine," Spider said, looking over at me while we waited for the exit gate to open.

"Wow," I responded, raising a brow. Beau had taken me to another restaurant by the same name in Paris. It had opened in the mid-sixties, but was more of a nightclub than a restaurant. I still had no idea how my husband had secured a reservation since it was the kind of place celebrities, dignitaries, and other billionaire types frequented.

The Miami Beach location was affiliated with the one in Paris, but I'd never been. I'd heard it was known as much for its dinner club as for the party scene it transitioned into at the stroke of midnight.

While I was a third-generation American, my family on my father's side was Russian—a fact Spider would've discovered in the dossier I had no doubt the FBI had provided him. How he knew I was a sucker for smoked fish, salmon roe, homemade blinis, and pavlova was a mystery. And maybe he didn't.

"Have you been before?" I asked as he navigated his way seemingly without a map, made more impressive because he knew to stay off the main drag, which would have turned the ten-minute drive into an hour.

"I haven't, but I've always wanted to."

When he pulled up to the entrance, two valets approached the car.

"I'll escort the lady," I heard him say to the man who opened the driver's door. Mine remained locked, to the apparent chagrin of the second guy.

"Welcome, Mr. Vaughn," the Russian-accented maître d' said when we walked through the door the second valet held open for us. "Please follow me. Your table is ready."

"I thought you said you've never been here before."

As with my comment about his car, Spider flushed. "I haven't."

I waited until we were seated and he'd accepted our host's offer of two shots from the bottle submerged in ice he'd set on the table, before I mentioned it. "You seem embarrassed."

"My mother and father are regulars."

"And?"

"I asked my dad to secure the reservation."

"Again, why does that embarrass you?"

He sighed, rested his arms on the table, and leaned toward me. "I try not to take advantage of my parents' largesse."

"Poor little rich boy?" I'd meant to tease him, but it fell flat. "Sorry," I mumbled.

"It's okay. It's just…I caught a lot of flack for it when I first joined the bureau. As if I wouldn't take my job seriously since my parents were wealthy. So, yeah, poor little rich boy."

The size of my bank account bothered me more than embarrassed me. The CIA had, for all intents and purposes, bought my silence after the circumstances of Beau's death were uncovered by the Invincibles, the team whose Christmas party I was refusing to attend. The current director of the agency, Kellen "Money" McTiernan, had arranged for the "settlement," not just for me but for all the families who'd lost loved ones during the years the intelligence community was rife with corruption and abuse of power.

Rounding out my net worth was the value of the house Beau had first inherited, then left to me. When his family had bought the land and built it, they probably paid under ten grand for it. Now it was worth upwards of five million, according to the most recent appraisal.

I realized I'd been lost in thought, but when I looked over at Spider, it didn't appear he'd noticed. Conversation, or lack of it, had been easy between us since we first met, and tonight was no different.

We quietly sipped our vodka—rather than downing it like a shot as was Russian tradition—each taking in the opulence of our surroundings. The dimly lit main room was awash in red. The bar and windows were backlit in the color, as were the chairs, tableclothes, and candles. The only things that differed were the carpeting, which was floral-patterned red and ivory, and the gold chandeliers with warm-white bulbs hanging above the tables. It was hard to imagine that in a few short hours, the space would be transformed from a restaurant to a dance club.

I studied the man sitting beside me. I couldn't explain my willingness to accept a friendship with Spider when my modus operandi was to push people away. Maybe it was because he never asked much of me besides company. Maybe it was because he sensed, like I had, that neither of us quite fit in with the team of agents with whom we'd worked our last mission.

Fitting in had never been easy for me, even before Beau's death. He'd once asked me what the hardest emotion for me to convey was. *Like* had been my answer.

With his sole exception, and now Spider's to a certain but different extent, I didn't let people in. I didn't desire friendships, either with people I worked with or outside of my job. I was perfectly happy being a loner. The only longing I did feel was for my dead husband.

I looked over and realized Spider was studying me. Too intently for my comfort.

"You look beautiful tonight, Casper."

I felt my cheeks flush and lowered my gaze. I wanted to punch his arm and tell him to knock it off, like I would've in seventh grade. Instead, I thanked him.

"You look nice too, Spider."

I'd definitely noticed how attractive he was the first time we met. Besides his height, he was as buff as any of the other agents I'd worked with during my time with the CIA and subsequently. While he looked nothing like Beau, there was something about his eyes—their warmth, I suppose—and the way his blond hair always looked like he'd just gotten out of bed that appealed to me on the same visceral level as my husband's appearance.

"I wish I knew what you were thinking," he said like he had so many times before. Typically, I had a snappy—or bitchy, as some considered it—comeback for him. Not this time.

"I'm wondering why you invited me to dinner."

"As I said, there's something I want to run by you."

2

Spider

Women didn't make me nervous. In fact, the vast majority annoyed me. Two rattled me, though. The first was Winslow Greer, a woman—really more of a girl when we were first introduced—I'd been on the Olympic ski team with. The second was Calla "Casper" Rey.

While Winslow had always been friendly, Casper was the opposite. And yet, her icy demeanor challenged me. The woman was hauntingly beautiful, with jet-black hair and intense violet-blue eyes the color of a blue jay's feathers. Her dominating personality also reminded me of the bird widely accepted as aggressive.

"Now, I wish I knew what you were thinking."

I blurted the first thing that came to mind when the last thing I wanted was to tell her I'd been mentally comparing her to a bird. "How'd you get your code name?"

"My husband."

Maybe it was the vodka I'd downed on an empty stomach lowering my inhibitions, but rather than respect her usually obvious unwillingness to talk about the man, tonight I asked the question I'd so often wondered. "Why?"

Her scrunched eyes bored into mine. Would she refuse to tell me? If so, I wasn't planning to let her off easy. I'd wait until she said as much or answered.

She huffed more than sighed. "He said I entered rooms silently, like a ghost."

"So why not Phantom or the Bell Witch or even Bloody Mary?" I teased.

"I don't know. Maybe he thought by referring to me by the name of a 'friendly' ghost, I'd become more so."

"It obviously worked. At least with him, since you were married." Something about her vulnerability spurred me to continue a topic of conversation she typically shut down before it began. Shamelessly, that vulnerability also turned me on. "How long did you know him before he proposed?"

I could feel her tension. "I don't remember."

I downed the vodka in my glass and poured another for each of us. "I don't believe you."

"What's with all the questions tonight?"

"I'm curious."

"Yeah, well, my marriage has nothing to do with why you invited me to dinner."

"Maybe it does."

Casper shot the vodka in her glass like I had. "Then, I'm not interested in hearing whatever it is."

"Fair enough." I studied the dinner menu.

"That's it? You invited me to dinner on the premise you had some kind of proposition for me, and because I won't delve into something that is none of your business, you drop it?"

I set the menu aside. "How long did you know each other before Beau proposed?" I repeated.

"Spider…"

"I told you my history with Winslow."

"It—she—was part of the investigation."

"My history with her wasn't. Especially the part about her refusing my marriage proposal. By the way, tonight is the anniversary of what I thought would be an engagement celebration. Instead, it became my utter humiliation."

"I'm sorry." Her hand crept toward mine, but she pulled it away before touching me.

"Don't be. We all know it was for the best."

Casper leaned against her chair, perhaps to distance herself from the temptation of comforting me. "You obviously loved her, or you wouldn't have proposed."

"I was an immature kid. So was she." I shrugged. "It's obvious now she was more interested in a ranch hand than a poor little rich boy." My words reflected a resentment I didn't feel. I was happy for Winslow and Cowboy. Particularly since her marriage to him meant my parents and hers would finally back off and stop encouraging me to pursue a renewed relationship with her.

"May I interest you in tonight's starter offering, freshly caught tuna tartare, or perhaps our signature Kaviari Kristal?" asked the waiter who'd approached our table.

"My father recommended allowing Aleksei to prepare a tasting menu for us tonight," I suggested to Casper, who hadn't looked at her menu yet.

When she nodded, the waiter did the same, removed our menus, and left the table.

"I'm not as much like my dad as I appear," I muttered, realizing I was coming across in the same way he would.

"I haven't met him to know."

I scowled. "He's a pompous ass."

When Casper laughed, I did too.

"Three weeks," she said, almost too quietly for me to hear. "We were married a week later."

I was flooded with humility and reached over to take her hand. She flinched, but I took it anyway. "Thank you for confiding in me."

She looked down at our hands on the table. "Spider, I don't want—"

I squeezed her fingers and let go. "A little comfort, Casper. We all need it from time to time."

"We got married on Christmas. I lost him before our fifth anniversary. Twenty-three days before." She blinked away tears I knew were unlike her to shed, particularly in front of anyone.

"Christmas sucks."

Her face broke into a smile. "You can say that again." Her grin faded. "The Invincibles are having a Christmas party. Attendance is mandatory."

I knew they were, and it was part of the proposition I wanted to run by her. "Are you going?"

"If you'd asked me that an hour ago, I would've said, 'fuck no.'"

I smiled. Calla hated cursing, when she wasn't the one doing it. I'd been on the receiving end of her annoyance enough times during the latest investigation to never forget how much it bothered her. "What changed?" I poured more vodka for each of us, and she rested her forearms on the table.

"I started thinking that if it weren't for them, I never would've known how Beau died. Irish Warrick suffered the disdain—maybe hatred is a better word—of everyone in the intelligence community when he went undercover on the mission that ultimately took down the ring of corrupt men responsible not just for Beau's death but countless others. I owe him. We all do."

"You'd consider going, out of respect for him?"

"Not just him. I mean, Decker Ashford and Rile DeLéon gave me my first assignments after I left the CIA. Keon Edgemon too."

I recognized the names of three of the four men who were the founding partners of the firm officially known as the Invincible Security and Intelligence Group. The fourth was Grinder Stone, a man I'd never met but admired as much as the other three.

She sighed. "They knew better than I did how much I needed to get back to work."

"From what I understand, they're all good men."

"Everyone who works with and for them is—men and women."

"Present company included," I said, winking.

Her eyes met mine, and in them, I saw gratitude rather than the anger from earlier. "Thanks."

"Housemade tarama with caviar Petrossian Osciètre," said the waiter as he set our first course on the table in front of us. *"Priyatnogo appetita."*

"He'd be fired for that in Moscow," Casper said under her breath when he walked away.

"Yeah? Why's that?"

She shrugged. "I'm not sure, except to say a 'servant' telling someone to enjoy their meal is considered presumptuous. Tarama is one of my favorites," she added, changing the subject.

"What is it?" I asked, studying the pink spread with the consistency of hummus.

"Cured roe, usually cod or carp, mixed with olive oil, lemon, and garlic."

"You're familiar with Russian customs as well as delicacies?"

"I started out in the CIA, as you know. If you're undercover in a particular country, you better be damned well versed in their etiquette."

"I wish I'd started out in foreign intelligence rather than domestic."

"I'm sure either the Invincibles or K19 would welcome you on their teams."

I'd met Casper while working with K19 Security Solutions and their second team, K19 Shadow Operations, on a recent investigation into serial kidnappings and murders in the Adirondack Mountains. I was assigned to the case when Winslow, the woman who'd turned down my marriage proposal, was kidnapped herself. The original intention had been for me to go undercover in the world of competitive skiing to see if she'd been abducted by someone affiliated with the sport.

Winslow had escaped her captor prior to the start of my assignment, but I'd stayed on as an investigator since I also had experience with a previous case headed up by the FBI's Violent Criminal Apprehension Program. That investigation had ended with the arrest and conviction of a man who, until then, was the most prolific serial killer in US history. While the exact victim count in the Adirondack case was still undeter-mined, I wouldn't be surprised if it took the top spot in terms of number of victims.

K19 had mentioned something about offering me a position with them whenever I decided to leave the bureau. However, given one of their senior agents had been college roommates with my boss at the FBI, it hadn't gone anywhere.

After reaching out to Decker Ashford to say I'd be interested in joining them if the opportunity presented itself, I'd received a call from Rile. He'd not only invited me to the Christmas party Casper mentioned, but he'd asked if I could convince her to attend as well. It sounded as though she was considering it without my prompting.

I pulled the bottle of vodka out of the bucket of ice and saw we'd already consumed half. Which meant rather than driving us home, I'd have to call for a car service to shuttle us to Casper's house, then find a place to spend the night, pick my car up in the morning, and return to Palm Beach then.

"Since I've already had too much to drive…" I said, pouring another glass for her and for myself.

Casper raised her glass in a toast. "It's really meant to be enjoyed with food."

"I'm currently familiar with the reason why."

She laughed. "Are you aware Russians tend to have greater trust in those with whom they've gotten drunk?"

"Is it working?"

"I told you how long Beau and I were together before he proposed, didn't I?"

"Does that mean you trust me, Casper?" I asked, no longer joking.

The smile left her face too. "I guess I do."

That would have to be good enough for now. And knowing Casper as well as I was beginning to, I recognized how hard that was for her to admit.

By the time the sixth and final course—pavlova—was served, there wasn't much vodka left in the bottle.

"Did we drink all that?" Casper asked when I held it up to check.

"I don't think it was full when he brought it to the table. However, I have no intention of driving." I checked the time and saw it was almost eleven. If we stuck around another hour, we'd find ourselves in the center of a dance club.

"I can call a car service," she offered.

"Already taken care of. They'll be here in about thirty minutes."

"I meant for me."

"I picked you up. I'll see you home."

"But—"

"And then I'll have the driver take me to a hotel, where I'll sleep off our delightful evening before picking up my car sometime tomorrow."

"You don't have to go to all that trouble."

I shook my head. "Please allow me to be the gentleman my mother raised me to be." I shook it again. "Actually, she had little to do with it."

"Your dad raised you?"

If I'd taken a drink of vodka, I would've spit it out. "Uh, no. They had nannies for that. Or I did."

Casper reached over and put her hand on my arm. "I'm sorry, Spider."

"Hey, I survived, right?"

It wasn't more than fifteen minutes before my cell buzzed with a message saying our driver had arrived. I excused myself, paid the tab, and swung into the men's room before returning to the table where Casper waited. "Ready?" I asked. When she nodded, I pulled out her chair and offered her my hand.

"Your nannies did a good job," she said, taking it.

We walked out of the restaurant that way, but as soon as we were outside, where the car waited, she yanked her hand away.

I knew Casper didn't feel about me the way I did for her. I wondered if she'd ever open up and let another man get close to her. The time she'd thanked me for being such a good friend to her, "almost like a brother," she'd added, felt like a knife in my heart. Until then, I'd believed we were getting closer. In fact, that night, I'd planned to kiss her when we returned to the camp—as cabins were called in the Adirondacks. Had she sensed it? Was that the reason she'd made it a point to tell me she looked at me the same way she would a sibling?

It hadn't stopped the way I felt about her, though. Calla Rey wasn't just pretty; she was hot as fuck. I'd lost count of the times I fell asleep to fantasies of having her in my bed instead of in one in a room down the hall.

She was tall, probably five feet ten or eleven. And while she was bodybuilder-competition toned, she was also curvy. It didn't matter that the dress she wore covered her from chin to ankles; it hugged her lushness in a way that had me on the edge of desire all night long. Now that I'd allowed myself to think about it, I'd moved to full-on, embarrassingly hard as a rock.

"You really don't have to do this," she said when I opened the back passenger door and motioned her inside.

"I really do," I said, sliding in beside her.

The drive back to Di Lido Isle, one of South Beach's Venetian Islands, took ten minutes. Five in, Casper's head was on my shoulder, and she was fast asleep. I hated waking her when we arrived at the gate, but I had to since I didn't know the code. Before I did, though, I leaned down and pressed my lips to her forehead. It wasn't the first time I had, either. Casper was one of those people car rides put to sleep if she was tired. I'd taken advantage of it each and every time it happened.

"Hey, sweetheart," I whispered. "We're back."

She jolted upright and surveyed our surroundings. "The code is 2328," she told the driver. It wasn't hard to figure out the numbers corresponded to her dead husband's name if typed into a keypad. It reminded me of how I'd changed my own the day I returned from Canada Lake to a house I rarely occupied.

I shook my head, chastising myself once again for falling for a woman there was no prayer would ever be interested in me. I couldn't help it, though. I'd missed her and had to see her.

It dawned on me then that we never got back around to the reason I'd invited her to dinner. My proposition. Given how tired she was and how much we'd both had to drink, I wouldn't bring it up now. If I did, I had little doubt she'd dismiss it out of hand without the slightest consideration. Maybe rather than returning to Palm Beach tomorrow, I'd wake up early, get a ride to Raspoutine to pick up my car, then swing by here and invite her to breakfast.

"I'll walk her in, then be right back," I said to the driver when he pulled up in front of her house.

"Wait," said Casper, putting her hand on my arm before I had a chance to get out.

"I'm walking you in. That's nonnegotiable, sweetheart."

"That wasn't what I was going to say."

"What, then?"

She leaned closer to me. "You don't have to find a hotel. You can stay here," she whispered.

"Are you sure about that?"

"Why not? I mean, we stayed in the same cabin for weeks, right?"

We had. And every night was torture for me. However, like then, I would do it again just because it meant I could be with her, close to her, a little longer.

I thanked the driver, got out, walked around the car, and opened her door, holding my hand out like I had at the restaurant. Also like then, I didn't let go until we reached the entrance to her house.

She started to enter a code into the keypad, but stopped.

"I'm not looking, if that's what you're afraid of."

"That isn't it."

"What, then?"

Casper turned her head toward me and did the very last thing I ever expected her to. She kissed me.

3

Casper

I don't know what possessed me to kiss Spider. I was all set to unlock the door, show him in, and lead him to the guest room. But he was standing so close, and he smelled so good, and he was so damned sweet and so fucking hot, I couldn't help myself.

Rather than pull away, like part of me feared he would, he cupped my cheek and deepened our kiss. How many times had I wondered how his lips would feel on mine? Too many to count. Then, though, I hadn't spent the evening drinking vodka, eating fabulous food, and enjoying Spider's company so much I hadn't wanted the date to end.

Maybe stone-cold sober, I would've talked myself out of being interested in him like I had so many times before. I might've reminded myself the house we were about to walk into was one I'd shared with my beloved husband.

Instead, I did none of those things. I focused all my attention on the way his tongue licked the seam of my lips before I opened to him and our mouths fused in frenzied desire. He lowered his hand and wrapped his arms around me. His fingers trailed down my spine, and he cupped the cheeks of my ass.

"Open the door, Calla," he said, kissing down the side of my face to where the collar of my dress covered my neck.

I entered the code, and we practically fell inside. Spider released me, closed the door, and when I set my bag on the table in the foyer, he stood behind me and wrapped his arms around my waist.

"God, you smell good," he said, breathing in as his head rested against mine.

"Spider—"

He dropped his arms and took a step back. "Sorry, I crossed the line—"

I turned around so I could see his face. "You didn't. I did."

He nodded and pulled his phone from his pocket, punching something on the screen.

"What are you doing?" I asked.

"Seeing if the driver's left the island yet."

Inexplicably, my eyes filled with tears. "Why?"

He looked up at me. "This isn't a good idea, sweetheart."

I felt my cheeks flame. "You're right. God, I'm so sorry."

He set his phone on the table, near my bag, and pulled me close to him. "Here's why it isn't a good idea. Now that I've finally kissed you, I don't want to stop."

"I can't. I mean, we can't."

He dropped his hands a second time. "I know, and that's why I can't stay."

A tear ran down my cheek. Fucking vodka. If I weren't drunk, I'd never cry in front of him. I wouldn't have kissed him either.

Spider wiped the tear away with the pad of his thumb. "Hey, now. There's nothing to cry about."

"I've ruined things between us."

"Do you really think it'll be that easy to get rid of me? I'd say you know me better than that."

"Then, why do you have to leave?"

He took a deep breath. "You know what? I don't. If you still want me to, I'll stay."

"Even though we can't…?"

He smiled and kissed my forehead. "Yep, even though we can't." He motioned toward the sofa. "Okay if I bunk there?"

"No. I have a bed. I mean, of course I have a bed. But I have two. Jesus. What I'm trying to say is I have a guest *bed*room." God, I was such an idiot. The last time I'd let my guard down this much was with Beau. My husband. My dead husband. I felt like banging my head against the wall. "I'm sorry, Spider. I think I passed the point of no return about two hours and five shots ago. I'm not like this. I mean, you of all people know I'm not like this."

"I do know, sweetheart. As much as I sometimes wish you were." He hung his head. "Forget I said that."

"I'm glad you said it," I whispered. "I won't be tomorrow, but tonight I am."

"Go to bed, Casper, and point me in the direction of mine. If you don't…"

"What?"

"I was going to say we both might fall over from exhaustion. However, that's not exactly true." He raised his head, and his eyes met mine. "If you don't, I might be tempted to kiss you again."

I wanted him to. So much. But like with me telling him I was glad he said what he had, I knew tomorrow, I wouldn't be. Tomorrow, I wouldn't be happy we'd kissed at all. I'd be mortified. I turned to walk away, but Spider grabbed my hand.

"In case this never happens again, I need one more."

I closed my eyes and squeezed his hand.

"Calla? Look at me."

I shook my head. "Just kiss me."

"Not until you look at me."

What I saw when I did nearly floored me. Beau was the only man who'd looked at me the way Spider was now. It was a night I remembered vividly because it was the last time we'd made love before he left on a mission he'd never return from. Whenever I thought about it, part of me wondered if he'd somehow known. That's how intense his desire had been. Just like Spider's was now.

Seeing it terrified me. Not because I was afraid of him, because I was afraid of how I felt when I was with him. Afraid of how much I wished I could lead him to my bed instead of down the hall to the guest room.

With his eyes focused on mine, Spider leaned forward and kissed me. He'd dropped his hands, so the only place we touched was our lips. I wished he'd put his arm around me so I could lean into him and feel his whole body against mine. And maybe that's why he hadn't. Because now I'd have to be the one brave enough to do it. I couldn't just let it happen or tell myself it wasn't what I wanted.

He drew away too soon. Long before I'd had enough, but his gaze didn't leave mine. It was as though he was challenging me to take more if I wanted it. I shook my head, turned, and walked away. I tried to tell him I wasn't brave enough, but he already knew that.

I stopped in front of the first door I came to and opened it. Spider joined me and peeked inside. "Looks like this is me," he said.

"Good night."

"Good night, Calla."

No one called me that anymore, not since my parents died. Everyone knew me as Casper. Even Beau hadn't called me by my given name. I liked how it sounded on Spider's lips, in his voice.

I kept walking until I reached the last door. Before opening it, I looked behind me. Spider was still standing on the guest room's threshold. When I raised my hand in a wave, he did the same.

I never slept well after I had too much alcohol, and tonight was no exception. I tossed and turned, woke up every hour at least, and by three in the morning, I had a pounding headache. By six, I forced myself out of bed and went into the kitchen to make a cup of coffee, drink a gallon of water, and wash down a couple of ibuprofens. When I heard another door open, I was glad I'd remembered I wasn't alone and had put a robe on before coming out of my room.

"Good morning," I said when Spider rounded the corner into the kitchen, surprised to see he was fully dressed. "I hope I didn't wake you."

He ran his fingers through his mussed hair. "No, I didn't expect you to be up."

Why did this have to feel so awkward? There were weeks of mornings when we met in the kitchen, me typically still in my flannel pajamas and him in sweatpants but no shirt.

I pointed to the coffeemaker. "I'm hoping caffeine will help. Can I get you a cup?"

He looked at the phone I hadn't seen in his hand. "No, thanks. I, uh, called a car service."

"At six in the morning?" *What the fuck?* "Were you trying to sneak out of here before I got out of bed?"

"I figured you wouldn't want to see me this morning."

"Why?"

"Maybe you don't remember—"

"I remember, Spider," I snapped.

"Don't get mad. I was trying to make it easier on you."

"The other thing I remember about last night is you saying I didn't ruin things between us."

His eyes scrunched. "You didn't."

"Then, why are you sneaking out of here like you never want to see me again?"

"That isn't what I'm doing."

When the coffeemaker sputtered, indicating it was done brewing, I poured a cup. "When's your ride supposed to be here?"

"Twenty minutes. I planned to walk up to the gate."

"Instead of waking me?"

"Come on, Casper. I really was trying to make it easier on you."

"Casper." I hated that he'd called me that instead of Calla.

"What?" His eyes met mine, and in them, I saw pain. And not the kind of hurt caused by a hangover.

I shook my head. "Nothing. You better go if you want to get to the gate in time. Have a nice life, Spider."

When I brushed past him to retreat to my bedroom, he grabbed my arm. "Don't do this."

"I'm not the one sneaking out of here. I'm not the one putting an end to our friendship. I'm not the one…" I had to stop talking. If I didn't, I'd cry, and the last thing I wanted was for him to see how much his actions hurt me.

"I'm not putting an end to our friendship."

"Right."

"I planned to leave before you got up, pick up my car, then call you later to see how you were feeling."

"Right," I repeated.

"And by later, I mean I planned to hang out in a coffeehouse or something until mid or late morning, then call to see if you felt good enough to meet for breakfast."

I pulled my arm from his grasp. "Bullshit."

"It's the truth."

"Goodbye, Spider." This time when I walked away, he rushed around me and kept me from getting to my bedroom.

"Please, Calla."

"Calla again, huh?"

"Dammit. I told myself I wouldn't do this, but you're giving me no choice."

"Do what? Leave and never look back?"

Spider took the cup out of my hand.

"And take my coffee with you?"

He returned to the kitchen, took a drink, set the cup on the counter, and stalked back to where I leaned against the wall. "No. This."

He put one hand around my waist, weaved his fingers in my hair with the other, then kissed me. He invaded my mouth with his tongue and pressed the full length of his body into mine. Exactly what I'd wanted him to do last night, but he hadn't.

At first, he was passionate, wild, and full of frenzied desire, then he eased off, and his lips felt reverent, gentle, almost hesitant. Impassioned or tender, both filled me with an emotion I couldn't name. With a cry in my throat, I kissed him harder, deeper, reclaiming the passion of a few seconds ago. I didn't want soft and sweet. I didn't want passivity. I wanted Spider to overwhelm me and leave me breathless with the need for more.

He gave me exactly what I'd hoped for. I could feel his hardness grow when he leaned in more, pressed himself against my abdomen, and moved his hand from my hair. He snaked it into my robe, pulled it open, and caught my aching nipple between his fingers, then he tore his lips from mine and lowered his head to take the other in his mouth.

"I've dreamed about doing this so many times," he said, moving his mouth to where his fingers had been. "Stop me, Calla. Tell me we can't do this. Tell me you don't want this."

My body was on fire, and I couldn't speak, even when he moved his hand between my legs and forced them open.

"Stop me, dammit," he said, parting my folds before thrusting one finger into my pussy while his thumb pressed against my clit. "Stop me or give me your pleasure, Calla," he said when my back arched and I writhed on his hand. I cried out when spasms racked my body while I held onto him as orgasmic waves crashed through me.

He hugged me tight, whispering my name, kissing my cheek, my neck, my shoulder as I floated back to earth. When my heart stopped pounding and my breathing returned to normal, Spider took a step back, closed my robe, and tightened its sash.

"I'll be back in an hour, sweetheart. Be ready to go out for breakfast so I can tell you what I intended to last night."

He didn't wait for me to respond before walking to the door, opening it, and leaving. I stayed where I was against the wall, but slid down it, landing on my bottom. I sat there, trying to conjure emotions I didn't feel. I should be aghast at my own behavior. Regretful for orgasming by the hand of a man who wasn't my husband. I should feel shame or even anger. I felt none of those things. In their place was anticipation. Of his return. Of breakfast. Of whatever he wanted to propose. Of more kisses. More of his hands and mouth on my body. Just more of him.

4

Spider

As much as I'd hoped that by the time I walked from Calla's house to the island's guardhouse, my erection would go away, it didn't. Thankfully, it was still early enough in the morning that I didn't encounter anyone out for a morning jog or getting the paper from their stoop, or even leaving in their car. I had to look exactly how I felt. Hungover, unbathed, walking about with little sleep, and sporting a not-so-little hard-on. It wouldn't surprise me if someone suspected a vagabond had sneaked onto their island. When I got to the gate, I walked under it and over to the waiting car.

"Corbin?" the driver asked.

"Yep," I answered, getting in the vehicle after confirming the make, model, and license plate matched what was on the app.

"You wanna go to Raspoutine?"

"That's right." I'd made arrangements last night for my keys to be put behind the bar and a note left for the cleaning crew, who Aleksei promised would arrive no later than five, letting them know I'd be coming by this morning to get them. Since there was no traffic, the ride from the island to the restaurant took a little over five minutes.

Because I had no idea what might happen with Calla as the day progressed, I picked up the keys, got in my car, then called a hotel I knew of a couple of blocks away on Ocean Drive and asked if they had any vacancies allowing for a *very* early check-in. I arrived a few minutes after confirming they did and gave the guy behind the desk a couple hundred bucks to have my clothes picked up from outside my room in five minutes, laundered, and delivered back to me as quickly as mechanically possible.

I inquired about the toiletries in the room and requested a toothbrush when one wasn't mentioned. The guy, who probably hadn't counted on a tip of that size first thing in the morning, went into the backroom and came out a minute later with a bag and a cup of coffee.

"I collected some extra things to make your stay more comfortable, sir," he said, handing both things to me. "Cream and sugar are on the sideboard behind you if you use them. Your clothes will be returned to you within forty-five minutes of you leaving them outside your door."

"There's another hundred in it for you if you can make it happen in under thirty."

"Yes, sir. You got it."

Once in my room, I removed my clothes, put them in the laundry bag I found in the closet, and set them outside my door. I brushed my teeth, took a shower, then donned one of the two robes I also found in the closet.

There was a pastry in the bag, which I set aside since I'd be taking Calla to breakfast, but I opened the pack of ibuprofen he'd given me and chased the pills with a full bottle of water. What I wouldn't do would be to sit or lie down. If I did, I might fall asleep, risking missing returning to Calla's place at the promised hour.

Twenty minutes later, there was a knock on the door. When I opened it, the same guy who'd been behind the front desk handed me my clean clothes. I reached into the pocket of the robe and gave him a hundred bucks. For the first time in my life, I was thankful for the undercover assignment I'd had in a Vegas hotel, when I learned how fast commercial machines could launder sheets and towels.

"I'd like to keep the room at least one more night if it's available," I said to my friend from the front desk.

"It's yours as long as you want it."

After thanking him and dressing, I rushed outside to my car the valet had parked and ready to go.

I arrived at the guardhouse with two minutes to spare, and while I knew the code, I wouldn't use it unless Calla told me to. I waited while the attendant called, relieved when he opened the gate a few seconds later. The insecure part of me worried she wouldn't answer, and if she did, she wouldn't let me back in.

I felt a sense of *déjà vu* when I parked in the same spot I had last night and walked to the door, wearing the same clothes. I knocked, then wiped my sweaty palms on my pants. Seconds later, the door opened and Calla waved me inside.

"I feel a little underdressed," she said.

I looked her up and down, loving how her snug jeans hugged her legs and how the black sweater she wore did the same to her curvy upper body. "You're perfect."

"Um, how?" she pointed at my clothes.

"I had a spare set in my car. And maybe I forgot to mention there's a bathtub in the trunk."

She laughed and shook her head. "Not that it's my business, but I'd love to know the real story."

"I've got a new friend at the Peabody on Ocean Drive. It's amazing how fast you can get a room and have your clothing laundered if you're willing to shell out a few bucks. God, I hate how much I just sounded like my dad."

Calla, as I was beginning to think of her, raised a brow. "Have you witnessed your dad after the walk of shame?"

I laughed. "No, but I have seen him grease more than a few palms to get something he wanted. So, uh, are you hungry?"

"Starving."

"Got a favorite breakfast spot?" I asked.

"Sure do."

"Lead the way."

Rather than walking toward the door, she approached the breakfast bar and pulled out a stool. "Have a seat."

I did as she told me and kept my eyes on her when she went around it and into the kitchen. "I make spectacular buttermilk pancakes, and I just so happen to have blueberries, raspberries, and fresh peaches."

I leaned against the stool and rubbed my stomach. "Sounds amazing. Can I help?"

"I've got it." She pulled a covered sheet pan out of the refrigerator, then turned on the oven.

"What's that?" I asked when she set it on the counter.

"You'll see. Coffee?"

"I'd love some." I thanked her after she set a cup on the bar, in front of me. I watched as she took a bowl and two different-sized pitchers, also covered, out of the fridge. She removed the lid from one and set it by the cooktop. When the oven beeped, she slid the baking sheet inside, lit a fire under the griddle, then poured pancake batter onto it from the largest pitcher.

While those cooked, she took the lid off the smaller of the two pitchers and stuck it in the microwave, then took the cover off the final bowl.

"Damn, woman, that smells amazing," I said when she removed the tray from the oven and a heavenly scent seduced my senses.

"Maple bacon. Not everyone likes it." She flipped the pancakes, then took the pitcher from the micro-wave and set it on the bar along with a bowl of fruit.

"There are forks, knives, and spoons in that drawer," she said, pointing with the spatula she used to transfer pancakes to two plates, which she also set on the bar.

I got out the utensils and set them between us. Following her lead, I put a spoonful of fruit on top of the pancakes, then poured warm syrup over it, groaning when I took a bite. "Damn, Calla, you never cooked when we were at the camp. This is amazing."

"The camp didn't have this kitchen. I got kind of spoiled."

Admittedly, although it was smaller, it was as nice as the one my parents had in their multi-million-dollar mansion.

"Forgot the bacon." She got off the stool, used tongs to put some on a plate, then set it between us.

We ate in silence, me because my mouth was continually full, her because she typically didn't feel the need to make small talk.

"Breakfast is fantastic. Thank you."

"You're welcome to have more."

"Don't twist my arm." Before she could get up, I did. "I'll get it."

I relit the griddle and let it heat up before pouring more batter from the pitcher. "Did you whip all this up while I was at the laundromat and bathing in the back of my car?"

She'd just taken a drink of coffee and covered her mouth when she laughed. "I just pictured you doing all that dressed like Magilla Gorilla."

"Tell me you looked it up online."

She giggled and nodded.

"See? Once you get that mental picture, it's impossible to forget it." I pointed to the griddle. "More?"

She held out her plate. "Two, please."

I put the rest on my plate after checking to make sure there was more batter, then sat beside her. "You didn't answer. Did you make all this while I was gone?"

She nodded. "I knew I wouldn't want to go out. So, what did you want to run by me?"

"A couple of things," I said, wiping my mouth with a napkin. "I think it's safe to say we have a similar dislike of Christmas."

Calla nodded again.

"And you mentioned the party the Invincibles are hosting. Have you given it any more thought? Going, I mean."

"I'm leaning that way. You aren't saying you want to go with me, are you?"

"Actually, I am."

She looked as though she was thinking about it. "Was that all?"

"Not by a long shot."

She leaned against the stool and folded her arms. "What else?"

"My parents have an annual New Year's Eve party at their place in Lake Placid."

"Yesterday, you said your proposition would benefit us both."

"I go to your party with you. You go to my party with me."

"What's the benefit?" she asked.

"One, we don't have to go alone. Two, by going together, neither of us has to pretend we like the holidays. You know, as we might have to with another plus one."

Calla unfolded her arms and took a bite of bacon. "Would we go as friends or as a date?"

"Whichever you'd prefer—"

"Friends."

That she said it before I'd finished my sentence stung a little. However, it was no secret, to me anyway, that Calla wasn't interested in me the same way I was in her. That I'd kissed her was more than I ever thought possible. This morning, when I used my mouth and hands to bring her to orgasm, it felt like a dream. If we were back to being "just friends," I'd accept it graciously. Or at least politely.

"I may be out of line here, but you don't seem like a huge fan of your parents. Or at least your dad. Why do you go, if that's the case?" she asked.

"Same reason you're thinking about attending the Invincibles' party. A certain amount of gratitude, I guess. While I'm not crazy about how my father flaunts his money, I never wanted for anything. No way I could've afforded competitive skiing without their support."

"I get that." She took another bite of bacon, then looked over at me. "I have a stipulation."

I almost said, "Lemme guess, no more kissing," but I kept my mouth shut, just in case that wasn't it.

"We each pay our own way."

My eyes scrunched. "Okay."

"Meaning you buy your own plane ticket to Texas; I buy my own to New York."

"Okay," I repeated. "Why is this a thing?"

"Last night, you paid the check before it even came to the table."

"So?"

"We've always split the check when we've eaten out together."

"The difference is last night I asked you to join me. You know, invited you."

"You're inviting me to your parents' party too."

"Fair enough. We each pay our own way. Anything else?"

When she shook her head, I breathed a quiet sigh of relief. At least, kissing—or more—wasn't *officially* off the table.

"The Invincibles' party is this coming weekend. And it's black tie," she reminded me.

"Not a problem."

"So…do you want to meet me there?"

"Is there a reason we can't travel on the same flight?" I asked.

"I guess not."

"Do you already have your ticket?"

She rolled her eyes. "I decided to go five minutes ago."

"Why don't we get them at the same time? That way, we can fly to Austin together, then from there to New York."

"But we have to come back here first."

We'd spent weeks together when we were working the investigation. What was the big deal now? If she didn't want to stay at my parents' place after leaving Austin, either she or both of us could get a hotel room or even rent a camp. "Sure, Casper. If that's what you want to do." I knew I sounded pissed off, because I was.

"Casper."

I looked up. "Why did you say your name'?"

"You called me Calla last night."

"And?"

"I liked it."

"Shit, Calla…Casper…whatever you want me to call you. One minute, you're saying we have to go dutch on everything and you want to go to both parties, but not spend any time together in between, then you're telling me you liked what I called you last night. You're giving me some major mixed signals."

Her cheeks flushed, and she looked away.

"I'm sorry for calling you out on it, but help me out here," I added.

"A little over a week separates the Invincibles' party and your parents'."

"Yeah?"

"Christmas is in between."

"You have big plans for it?" I asked.

"No, but…"

"But what?"

"Don't you want to spend it with your family?"

I knew what I was about to say might make Calla call off both parts of our arrangement, but I couldn't keep up the charade of her not mattering as much to me as she did. I drew in a fortifying breath, let it out slowly, then looked into her eyes. "I'd rather spend an ordinary day with you. Maybe get Chinese takeout or go for a boat ride. Hell, we could even go to an amusement park." I waited for her response, watching her eyes dart between mine.

"Okay."

"Okay?"

She cocked her head and smiled. "Yes, Spider."

5

Casper

After he helped me with the dishes, Spider and I sat down at the bar with our laptops, agreed on which flight to take to Austin, then individually purchased the tickets.

"Wait, what seat did you choose?" he asked.

"I always sit in the exit row."

"The exit row?"

"More legroom." I looked over at his screen. "What are you doing?"

"Changing my ticket."

"Why?" I asked before the reason dawned on me. "You're flying first class, aren't you?"

"No," he said, turning the screen more so I couldn't see what he was doing.

"Liar."

"I just assumed we would, that's all." His cheeks turned pink like they had last night. I couldn't understand why he got so flustered about having money. He said he caught a lot of slack about it at the bureau, but this seemed like more than that.

"Don't change because of me. Since I'm comfortable in an exit row and wouldn't eat on a plane anyway, I don't see any reason to spend the extra money. You do you, and I'll do me."

"It's a three-and-a-half-hour flight."

"Exactly. It'll be over before you know it. Ready to work on the other tickets?"

"Yeah, give me a sec."

I stood and looked over his shoulder. "Spider! What are you doing? Don't fly economy just because I am."

"I want to sit with you."

I rolled my eyes and sat down. "You're being ridiculous. If it means that much to you, I'll switch."

"No, it's okay. I've already changed it. Just tell me what row and seat you're in," he said.

"I'm in 15C."

"Great. B is open."

"But that's the middle seat. You're six-three."

"You said it's the exit row. More legroom."

"You've never flown economy, have you?"

He sat back and folded his arms. "What's your point?"

"Why does it bother you so much? I know you said you caught shit for it at the bureau, but this feels more like an overreaction."

He leaned forward and rested his arms on the bar. "I don't know. It's always been that way, I guess."

"Why?"

He closed his eyes and raised his face to the ceiling. "Can we change the subject?"

"Sure." I closed my laptop, got up, and went out to sit by the pool.

Spider followed a few seconds later.

"I kind of get it," I told him as I took off my shoes, rolled up my jeans, and stuck my feet in the water.

"You do?"

"I have a lot of money, Spider. More than I can ever spend in my lifetime."

He sat down beside me but didn't say anything.

"You think having it bothers you? Mine is blood money."

"I'm sorry, Calla. I feel even worse now."

"That's the thing. I'd give it all back in a heartbeat if it meant Beau was sitting here beside me. But that can't happen any more than you can change the fact your family is wealthy."

"The plane ticket drove it home. I didn't earn the money I have. If I had to live on my salary, I couldn't do it. I mean, this morning, I tipped a guy three hundred bucks to get my clothes washed so I could get back here in an hour. Three hundred bucks!"

I bumped him with my shoulder. "Instead of calling me to say you'd be by later. Better yet, you could've just stayed."

"See? God, I'm such an asshole."

"You're not an asshole, Spider. If you were, I'd be the first to call you out on it."

"Ain't that the truth?" He laughed, and I nudged him with my shoulder again.

"Next time, just let me wash your clothes."

"Will there be a next time, Calla?"

"Maybe not with that much vodka."

"What about that much kissing?"

"I'm not sure."

"I shouldn't have said that, and not just because it sounded stupid." He shook his head. "There's something I need to tell you."

"Go ahead."

"I talked to Rile. Before him, I talked to Decker."

"What about?"

"I told Ashford I'd be open to working with them if the opportunity presented itself."

"How did that turn into a conversation with Rile?"

"He called and asked me to help get you to the party."

"You didn't. I mean, I decided to go before you offered to join me."

"I know. I just didn't want you to think I was trying to pull something."

That he admitted it, meant a lot to me. Behind his penchant for self-deprecation was a really good guy. I leaned over and kissed his cheek. "Thanks for telling me."

When he lay back on the pool deck, I did the same. The next thing I felt was his fingers brushing mine.

"I really like you, Calla. I don't want to mess things up between us."

I turned to my side so I was facing him. "I lost Beau four years ago. To some, that may seem like a long time."

"But it isn't to you."

"Last night—this morning—I don't want you to think I'm ready to move on yet."

"Yet?"

"I didn't misspeak."

"I guess I can hang with that."

I shook my head and laughed. "I haven't done much of that in the last few years."

"Hang?"

"Laugh. You disarm me—in a good way. Not many people do."

He turned to his side like I had. "I love making you laugh."

I held my breath for a minute before slowly blowing it out. "For the most part, I've spent four years alone. It's going to take me a minute to get used to spending time with anyone outside of work."

"I can be patient, Calla."

As much as I wanted to lean in and kiss him, I wasn't sure I could say the same thing.

We reached a compromise for the trip to Lake Placid. Since we were both flying economy to Austin, we agreed to splurge for first class to New York. After our tickets were booked, and before Spider left to return to Palm Beach, he asked if he could take me to dinner again the night before our flight to Texas for the Invincibles' party.

"Just so there's no miscommunication, you can stay here—in the guest room—that night," I said.

He winked. "Guest room, my room, same difference, right?"

This man could make me smile like no other ever had, including Beau. As soon as the thought crossed my mind, a horrible feeling settled in my stomach.

"What just happened?" Spider asked.

"On second thought, you should probably get a hotel room that night."

He put his hands on my shoulders. "I can do that, but tell me what made you do a one-eighty."

I took a step backwards. "It just isn't a good idea for you to stay here."

He dropped his hands and slowly nodded. "More than anything, I'm your friend, Calla. Talk to me. Tell me what's going on. If I'm doing something that makes you uncomfortable, say so."

Could I? Wasn't I already giving this man so many mixed signals his neck would surely snap? Physically, I was so attracted to him it was hard for me not to touch him if he was within reach. I enjoyed his company more than anyone since Beau. But as far as making me smile, making me laugh, Spider did more often than I remembered my husband doing, and that, along with the physical stuff, felt like betrayal.

"You lost your husband four years ago, and you're not ready to move on from your relationship with him. I heard you loud and clear when you said that earlier, sweetheart. I promise I won't push for more than you're able to give or more than you're interested in."

I studied him. There had to be a long line of women interested in a relationship with Spider. Women who were younger, more attractive, not stuck between moving on and staying loyal to their dead husband. "Why me?" I whispered.

He shook his head. "You feel the connection as much as I do. Whether you're ready for it or not is the question. However, there's no denying the chemistry between us. If you do, you're lying."

"But—"

"If I thought for one minute this thing was one-sided, I wouldn't be here. I've been there and done that, remember? There's no way I'll set myself up for similar heartbreak."

"What if I'm never ready?"

He scratched the side of his head. "I'm not sure I want to answer."

"Why not?"

"You're either going to think I'm a pompous ass or full of shit. Maybe both. I also don't want you to think I won't respect your wishes to take things slow."

"But?"

He walked away, turning to face the window.

"Spider? Just tell me."

He looked up at the ceiling and shook his head. "I'm so afraid I'm going to regret saying this."

"Do it anyway."

He turned around, lowered his head, and looked into my eyes. "You're more ready than you think you are." He walked closer and rested his hand on my heart. "Here." He moved the same hand up to cup the side of my head. "It's here you're telling yourself you aren't."

6

Spider

For both our sakes, I decided to leave shortly after we'd finished purchasing our plane tickets. Even if Calla had asked me not to, I knew we both needed time and space to sort through our feelings. If I'd stayed a moment longer, I wouldn't have been able to stop myself from saying the one thing Calla was definitely not ready to hear. I was in love with her. That much was undeniable.

Instead of taking her to dinner the night before we left for Texas, like I'd originally hoped, I told her I'd meet her at the airport today before our flight. While I typically arrived at the airport with over an hour to spare, not wanting to risk hitting traffic between Palm Beach and Miami, now I was faced with more than two hours to kill.

I was about to sit at the bar of an airport restaurant when I saw Calla heading toward our gate, rolling a carry-on beside her, and wearing a pair of jeans, a snug black sweater, and black boots.

"Can I get that for you, miss?" I said, walking up behind her.

She spun around and put her hand on her heart. "Hey, Spider."

"Sorry if I startled you. I was about to get breakfast when I saw you walk by."

"I'm starving. Mind if I join you?"

"I'd love it. Bar or table?" I asked.

"Bar's good with me."

I leaned forward and kissed her cheek. "It's nice to see you, Calla."

She smiled. "It's nice to see you too."

We both ordered coffee when the bartender dropped off menus. The buttermilk pancakes sounded good, but I doubted they'd come close to the ones Calla made. I decided on eggs and bacon and set the menu down.

"Would you mind if I have a drink?" she asked.

"Of course not. What would you like?"

Calla rolled her shoulders. "A Bloody Mary."

"I could go for one of those myself."

When the bartender approached, I ordered two, then waited for Calla to order her breakfast. When she chose the pancakes, I was surprised but asked for the same thing.

When the man walked away, I sensed her tension. "Anything I can help with?"

"Call Rile for me and tell him I caught a last-minute flight to Fiji?"

I smiled. "Fiji versus Austin. Hmm. Mind if I go along?"

"Both of us would end up on his shit list if we did. Decker's too."

"Probably wouldn't offer me a gig either. By the way, maybe I should've asked if you minded."

"Minded what? That you let Decker know you'd be interested in contracting with them?"

I nodded.

"Of course not. You're a good agent, Spider. They'd be lucky to have you on board."

"Cheers," I said when our drinks appeared. We clinked glasses and each took a hefty sip.

"Spider?" I heard a voice say from behind me.

When I turned around, I didn't recognize the woman who'd said it. "Hi," I said, hoping she'd tell me her name or at least how she knew me.

"You don't recognize me, do you?" she asked.

"Sorry. Too many skiing accidents involving head injuries, I guess. Remind me your name?"

"Danielle Sweeney. My mom is Susan Sweeney."

I still couldn't place the name.

"Leopard?"

"Oh. Wow. You're Leopard's daughter? It's, uh, nice to see you." I couldn't remember the last time I saw her mom, and I sure couldn't remember ever meeting Danielle. "Um, tell your mom I said hey."

The young woman—who I now realized couldn't be out of her teens—left, and when I turned around, Calla was grinning, arms folded. She shook her head.

"What?"

"You don't remember me, do you?" she mimicked.

"I haven't skied competitively in years." I counted on my fingers. "And it's probably been at least twelve since I last saw Leopard, err, Susan. How old would you guess Danielle was at the time? Three or four, tops? Probably younger."

"And yet she remembers you."

"To be fair, you'd just said my name, and the kid probably saw photos of me from back in the day, given her mom and I were on the ski team together."

"Were you in a relationship with her mother?"

I put my arm on the back of her barstool and leaned closer so my mouth was next to her ear. "Why do you ask, sweetheart?" When she didn't respond, I inhaled her scent. "Damn, you smell good."

Calla's breath hitched, and I could see her nipples pebble under her tight sweater. When she turned her head and faced me, she was so near if I got another couple of inches closer, I could kiss her.

"I missed you," I blurted before I had the chance to talk myself out of it. I closed the distance between us halfway to see what she'd do, and was stunned when she met me in the middle.

"I missed you too," she whispered before her lips brushed mine.

"If we weren't in the middle of a crowded bar in an equally crowded airport, I would kiss the hell out of you, sweetheart."

Calla leaned in again, this time pressing her tongue against my lips. I opened them to her. While brief, our kiss held more promise than I'd expected. Truth be told, I'd anticipated spending tonight and tomorrow stuck firmly in the friend zone. I'd refrain from getting my hopes up, though. Maybe once we were in Austin, that was exactly where I'd land.

We each had another drink, then went to the gate. We were only there for a few minutes when I heard our names called. "I'll go," I said, walking up to the desk.

"Mr. Vaughn?"

"That's me."

"I wanted to let you know you've been upgraded to first class."

I groaned. "I have been? Why?"

"I can't say."

"What about Calla Rey? She and I are traveling together."

"She has been as well. You're in seats 3E and 3F."

The woman handed me the new boarding passes.

"You aren't going to believe this, but we've been upgraded. And no, I had nothing to do with it." I handed the piece of paper to her.

Calla raised a brow.

I sat beside her. "Look, if I had, I'd say so. I swear."

"My guess is Rile did this. Or Deck."

"How?"

"If you don't know how, I'm certainly not going to be the one to tell you."

I had heard there wasn't a firewall on the planet Decker Ashford couldn't get beyond. If that included hacking into the airline, I wasn't sure I wanted to know.

Once boarded, Calla insisted she preferred the window over the aisle, and we settled into our seats.

"Ms. Rey, Mr. Vaughn?" said the flight attendant.

"Yes," I responded.

"This is courtesy of…" She looked at her phone. "The Invincibles?"

"Thank you," I said when she handed each of us a glass and a bottle of Veuve Clicquot—my champagne of choice.

"This is my favorite," Calla said when I poured a glass for each of us.

"Mine too," I said, smiling.

"This answers the question of who's responsible for the upgrade."

"Decker?"

Calla shook her head. "Rile."

I raised a brow. "What makes you so certain?"

"He knows," she responded, pointing to the bottle.

I was well aware Rile was a happily married man. However, that he knew Calla's favorite champagne irked a little.

"It's actually his wife, Kenzie, who knows. She must've told him."

I smiled and she studied me.

"Tell me you weren't jealous."

I shrugged a shoulder, clinked her glass, and sipped my champagne. If we polished off this bottle on top of the two drinks we'd had at the bar, we'd both be a little tattered when we landed three hours from now. A little drunk was okay. Shit-faced, like we both were the night we went to Raspoutine, wasn't.

Calla's cheeks turned pink. "I should've run this by you but when Rile me asked about accommodations, I told him we were traveling together."

I wasn't sure how to respond.

"We'll be staying in a guesthouse on King-Alexander Ranch," she continued.

"Okay."

"It's one of the smaller houses, so no one else will be with us."

"Okay," I repeated. Surely, given my education, I could've come up with something more or better to say, but I didn't.

"Is that all right with you?"

"Of course. Why wouldn't it be?"

She rested against her seat. "I know I'm not being fair to you."

"Let me be the judge of that."

"I told you I didn't want you to stay with me last night."

I could see nothing good coming from this conversation. "Do you want to know how I feel about it? What I think?"

"I do."

I turned my body, cupped her cheek with my hand, and kissed her. It was the kind of kiss I hadn't felt comfortable giving her in the bar in the middle of the airport. However, since we were in our own row and most people were too busy filing in and looking for their seats—not to mention, I really didn't give a shit who saw us—I didn't hesitate to deepen the kiss when Calla responded by putting her hand on my arm.

"I told you it was him," I heard the same voice as at the bar say from behind me. This time, I ignored her. At least until I heard someone clear their throat—twice.

I broke away and looked over my shoulder.

"Uh, hey, Susan."

"Spider," she all but spat.

If she was going to be a bitch, why had she bothered clearing her throat? Not to mention, her daughter had continued walking down the aisle while her mother held up the passengers waiting behind her.

"I didn't think I'd ever see you again. I guess I should've figured it would be a chance meeting," she huffed.

"Ma'am, either step out of the way or continue your little reunion after the plane is in the air," said the man standing behind her.

She huffed again and walked away.

"What was that all about?" Calla asked.

I shook my head, eyes wide. "No clue."

"You never answered my question."

I leaned against my own seat, dazed. "Which one?"

"Were you ever in a relationship with her?"

"I wouldn't define it as a relationship."

"But you had sex with her?"

I nodded.

"More than once?"

"A few times."

"And yet, you didn't remember her name."

"Hold up a sec," I said, turning to face her. "I'd be willing to bet she doesn't remember mine either.

I never knew her as Susan, and she sure as hell didn't know me as Corbin. No one did."

"What she said about thinking she'd never see you again was odd."

"The whole thing was odd."

"Spider, how old were you the last time you were 'with' her?"

7

Casper

When he didn't respond right away, I knew he was doing the math the same way I was.

"I was eighteen."

"So, what? Fourteen years ago? I'm assuming she didn't have a child then."

He shook his head.

"Could the daughter be yours?" I asked.

His eyes scrunched. "No. I might've been a kid, but I sure as hell wasn't an irresponsible one. I knew what was at stake."

"Meaning?"

"The Olympics. For both of us. Not that she made the final cut." He put his head in his hands. *"Fuck."* He looked at me with wide eyes. "Sorry for cursing."

"It's okay. But why did you?"

"She dropped out." He lowered his hands. "If she got pregnant, I wasn't hard to find. Especially if that's why she quit. She could've talked to me any time she wanted to."

"No one would've restricted her access?"

"I don't know who would have. She was on the team. There's no way I could be the kid's father. No way she wouldn't have told me." He leaned forward and rested his head against the seat in front of him, then turned and looked at me. "What did the girl say her name was?"

"Danielle?"

He sat upright. *"Fuck,"* he repeated under his breath. "Sorry."

"Stop apologizing. I get it. Why'd you say it this time?"

"We call my brother Dein, short for Deiniol—Welsh for Daniel."

I remembered reading Spider had a brother, but I couldn't recall his age or even whether he was older or younger. "Do you think…"

"It wouldn't surprise me."

"Why would she be so hostile to you?" I asked.

"Family connection? And before you ask, Dein can be just as much of an asshole as my father." Spider shook his head. "This would be just like him."

"What do you mean?"

"Dein made a play for Winslow. She shut him down pretty damn quick. Not that it stopped him from trying again."

"What's the age difference between you?" I asked.

"He's two years older."

"Danielle asked if you recognized her. Does she look like him?"

He shrugged. "I'd have to get a better look. Someone else had all my attention." He smiled, took my hand, and brought it to his lips. "Thanks, Calla."

"What for?"

"Not jumping all over me for this. Not just assuming the kid could be mine."

"I don't know you that well, Spider, but it seemed out of character."

"Again, thanks." He motioned to the bottle of champagne. "Do you want any more of this?"

"Not right now."

"Me, either. Would you mind if I told the flight attendant to share it?"

"Are you suggesting she offer it to Susan?" I asked.

Spider laughed out loud. "I was thinking to the other passengers in first class, but you may be onto something."

"You may want to consider being preemptive."

"Meaning attempt to talk to her before she does?"

"You might avoid an unpleasant scene if you do."

"Because there's so much privacy on an airplane?"

I motioned to two rows ahead of us. "If that seat remains empty, I'll sit there while you invite her here so the two of you can chat."

"Thanks, Calla." He got up and took the bottle of champagne with him. "I'm gonna kiss you again," he said when he returned empty-handed. "Are you all right with that?"

"More than all right."

We kissed until the plane taxied to the runway and sped up to take off. When it did, he held my hand, just like Beau used to.

I closed my eyes and thought about the words Spider had said the last time I saw him. I'd spent a lot of time thinking about them between then and now.

"You're more ready than you think you are," he'd said, putting his hand on my heart, then adding that my brain was what was telling me I wasn't.

I also thought about Beau and me after Spider left that day. If it had been me who'd died, the last thing I would've wanted was for him to live the rest of his life without love. As soon as I thought about it that way, I knew he wouldn't have wanted me to be alone, either.

Like Beau and me, Spider and I became friends first. He was caring, smart, made me laugh, and was an all-around good guy. I knew it in my heart. He'd thanked me for not immediately jumping to the conclusion he'd fathered a child he didn't know about, and even though I'd asked if Danielle could be his daughter, something inside was telling me she wasn't.

"This is going to sound like it's coming out of left field."

"Go ahead," he said.

"Have you ever thought about having children?"

"Yeah. I've thought about it. You?"

"Beau and I talked about it before he died. We weren't ready at the time."

"Do you wish you'd had a baby with him?"

I shrugged. "I don't know. I mean, I would've loved to have a part of him to hold onto. Loved to see glimpses of him in a baby he and I made together, but it would've been so hard for that child to grow up without knowing his or her father."

"Have you thought about it since?" he asked.

"Not a lot, except I know I'd like to be a mom. If I found someone I loved enough to raise a family with."

I waited for Spider to tell me whether he wanted to have kids, but when he didn't say anything, I didn't ask. Instead, I closed my eyes, not really feeling like delving into another conversation.

"Hey, Calla," I heard him whisper a few minutes later.

I opened my eyes. "Yeah?"

"I want a family too. With someone I love."

I squeezed his hand and closed my eyes again. When the pilot announced he was turning off the seat belt sign, I nudged Spider with my elbow. "Now's your chance."

"You really think I should do this?"

"Like I said, you might want to strike before she has the chance. Something tells me she intends to."

When Spider got up and walked toward the rear of the plane, I stood and walked toward the front, where the entire first row on one side was empty. "Would it be okay if I took that seat for a few minutes?" I asked the flight attendant.

"Go right ahead. Would you like more champagne?"

"Thanks, but I think I'll wait a bit."

"You've got it."

I glanced behind me and saw Spider return to our seats. Susan followed. I shifted over to the spot by the window, took my noise-canceling earbuds out of my pocket, put them in, and shut my eyes again. I must've dozed off, but I woke when I felt a hand on my arm.

"How'd it go?" I asked Spider, removing my earbuds.

"Incredibly awkward."

"Meaning?"

"She assumed I knew. Still thinks so."

"Is your brother…"

He nodded. "She didn't confirm or deny it using those exact words, but from what I gathered in the little she said, she was given a significant amount of money to raise her baby on her own—without 'the father's' involvement."

"Would your brother do that?"

"It wouldn't surprise me. It also wouldn't shock me if I learned my dad was behind it."

"Why wouldn't he and your mom want to be involved in their grandchild's life?"

"Oh, they are. Just not that grandchild. I asked Susan how old Danielle is. She's thirteen."

I raised a brow.

"She looks older, right?" he said.

"To be honest, I can't gauge it very well."

"Me neither. Anyway, what I was going to say is, *coincidentally*, my brother has been married almost thirteen years to a woman whose parents are good friends with ours. They have been most of our lives."

"Jesus," I muttered.

"I know."

"So, what's your mother like?" I asked, figuring I might as well get the lay of the land with his family all at once.

"She's not like my dad, but she doesn't stand up to him. He rules the roost, as they say."

"You're so unlike him. How did that happen?"

"I can be. Even though I try hard not to. Every once in a while, I catch myself, and it makes me sick."

"You're too hard on yourself."

"I was an asshole when Winslow first escaped the kidnapper. Her parents called and asked me to step in. I tried, but it was obvious right away she felt safer with

Cowboy. More than she did with me. I got pretty mad about it, left the police station, and thought about not coming back."

"What made you change your mind?"

"I swear to God it was hearing my father's voice in my head telling me to go back and insist I be the one to take over with whatever was happening with Winslow at that particular time."

"So you did the opposite?"

"Exactly."

"Who are you like? It doesn't sound like either of your parents."

"Kip. He was my ski coach from the time I was little. I think I started skiing with him when I was eight. He gave me the nickname Spider. Anyway, to be really good—good enough to make the Olympic team—you have to train year-round. I spent more time with Kip than I did with my parents and Dein. I wasn't unique. Most skiers were like that."

"I got the impression Winslow didn't spend much time with her parents when she was growing up."

"Yeah, her mom and dad are a lot like mine. They definitely wanted her and me to end up together. I sure am glad we didn't."

"Why not?" I asked.

"Winslow belongs with Cowboy, not me."

I would ask whom he belonged with, but I knew what he'd say. Or at least I thought I knew. I wasn't quite ready to confirm it, though.

"Why did Kip start calling you Spider?"

"I was skinnier than shit. He said my arms and legs looked as long and gangling as a spider's."

"And it stuck."

"Code names aren't as important at the bureau."

I shrugged. "Beau is the one who started calling me Casper. I already told you that. Anyway, it stuck, like Spider did with you."

After we landed in Austin, I received a message from Rile, saying Steel was waiting in the arrival lot and to text him as soon as we got off the plane. Once he picked us up, he'd take us to King-Alexander Ranch to get settled before tonight's party.

"I'm glad you're here with me. I mean, I know you're here on your own, but you traveled with me. I'm glad of that." I rolled my eyes at how stupid I sounded. This was why I preferred to keep my mouth shut. "Better to remain silent and be thought a fool than to speak and remove all doubt," as my mother used to say.

Spider put his arm around my shoulders and pulled me close to him. "I'm glad I'm here with you too."

I sent Steel a text, letting him know which door we were closest to. A few minutes later, a black SUV pulled up. He got out and stalked toward us.

"*What* is that?" asked Spider.

"*What?* Do you mean who? That's Steel."

"Holy shit," I heard him mutter under his breath.

"I forgot you haven't met him yet."

8

Spider

I wasn't a little guy. Hell, I was six-three and weighed in around two-twenty. However, as I watched "Steel" walk toward us, I felt like that skinnier-than-shit kid I was just telling Calla about.

The guy had to be at least six inches taller than me and carried another thirty pounds of pure muscle. His long dark hair hung inches past his shoulders, and he had one of those beards that probably always looked to be the perfect length yet not groomed. Fuck, I was as straight as an arrow, and *I* thought the guy was hot as hell.

When he wrapped his arms around Calla, picked her up, and spun her around before setting her on her feet, every bone in my body turned possessive. But what was I going to do about it? Kick him in the shin?

"Steel, this is Spider," she said, pulling the hulk over to me. His hand engulfed mine when he shook it, and the way his icy blue eyes bored into mine, I felt certain he intended to come across just as menacing as he was.

"So, uh, you work for the Invincibles?" I asked.

"Yeah, Edge recruited me. Before that, I was a bouncer at the Branch." He nudged Calla. "That's when I met this one." He slung his arm around her shoulders and glared at me. "So, Rile mentioned you were coming to talk to him and Deck about a job. What's your background?"

Calla laughed, elbowed him in the side, and stepped out of his reach. "Knock it off, Steel."

"What?" he said, laughing and holding both hands in the air.

"You're our ride, not the advance party."

"The advance what? The party isn't until later, darlin'."

Calla looked in my direction and rolled her eyes.

Okay, so he wasn't the smartest guy who'd ever kicked a few assholes out of a bar. Still, he was intimidating as hell.

"This is where Cowboy and Winslow stayed. I guess Mayhem was here for a while too," Steel said when he pulled into a driveway after we'd gone at least a couple of miles beyond the ranch's main entrance. "Shredder and I are next door. I can't remember whether Deck said Buster was bunkin' with us or you."

"With you and Shredder," Calla said, getting out of the SUV before either Steel or I could open the door for her. Probably for the best, since if I'd beat him to it, he might've leveled me while pushing me out of the way. "We're riding over with Rile and Kenzie," she added before waving at Steel and motioning for me to follow her into the house.

"This is nice," I said after she placed her hand on a pad by the door and it sprung open.

"The house or its security?" she asked.

"Uh, both."

"You know who owns King-Alexander, right?"

I raised a brow and cocked my head. "Yes, *Casper*."

She laughed. "Sorry. God, Steel makes me crazy."

"In a good or bad way?"

"You're kidding, right? 'The advance what? The party isn't until later, darlin','" she mimicked. "Sometimes I wanna smack him upside the head to see if any brain cells shake loose. Problem is, I can't reach his damn head."

I leaned against the kitchen island. "Come here."

When she took a step closer, I took her hands in mine.

"How are we playing this tonight? Agents who worked the Thanatos investigation together and just happened to both be traveling from Miami to Austin?"

"If you think Decker or Rile believe we just *happened* to be traveling from anywhere, you're in the wrong line of work."

"Okay. Friends, then? I don't want us to come across as something you'd rather we didn't."

"How would we do that?"

I shrugged. "I heard a rumor there might be dancing."

Calla leaned her body into mine.

"You keep that up, and we won't make it to the party, let alone the dance floor, sweetheart," I warned, wishing I could wrap my arms around her, squeeze the luscious cheeks of her ass, and pull her close enough that she could feel how much I'd rather stay here alone with her for the rest of the night. I let go of her hands, and she took a step back.

"Let's just be two people at a party together," she said.

"We can do that."

"It's hard to imagine everyone together in one place."

"I got the impression this was really important to Rile."

"If it weren't for him, there wouldn't be an Invincible Intelligence and Security Group. Especially since no one would've agreed to the name if he hadn't insisted."

I chuckled. "Decker, Edge, and Grinder couldn't talk him out of it?"

"It's pretty hard to change Rile's mind if he has it set on something. Case in point, I'm here instead of Fiji."

"Hmm. Maybe instead of an amusement park, that's where we should go for Christmas."

"You'd never get me to leave in time for your parents' party."

"All the better," I said with a wink. "Oh, and why are we riding to the party with Rile?"

"He sent a message, a few minutes ago, saying he wanted to talk to both of us beforehand and would meet us here."

I checked my phone and saw I'd received the same text Calla had. "Copy that."

She raised a brow. "Everything okay?"

"To be honest, I'm not sure. A few days ago, it seemed like a really good idea to reach out to Ashford to discuss an opportunity to work with his team. Now, I'm feeling out of my element."

She walked farther into the house and sat down on a sofa. When she waved me over, I joined her.

"I've felt—still feel—out of my element with this crowd too. But at the end of the day, they call me when an assignment they need help with pops up. I don't call them. When I told Rile I wouldn't be coming to the Christmas party, he wouldn't take no for an answer. When I last spoke with him, he said they're adding another team and they want me to partner. Fury Storm and Vex Dunning are heading it."

"That's great. I'm happy for you, Calla."

"I wouldn't be at all surprised if that's what Rile wants to talk to you about too."

I, on the other hand, would be. "Maybe. Would you have to relocate?"

She shrugged. "That might be a dealbreaker for me. What about you?"

"I'm not even sure they want me on board as a contractor."

Calla slapped her knees. "Guess we'll find out tonight. Maybe we should get ready."

I suggested she make use of the master bedroom and took one of the smaller guest rooms for myself. After unpacking my tux, I took a long, hot shower, hoping it would settle me. I wasn't used to feeling nervous over a job opportunity. Was that really what was behind my anxiety, though? More likely, it was the woman currently changing her clothes in the other bedroom.

The idea she might be getting out of the shower and walking naked to her bed, where she'd laid her clothes out, made me hard as a fucking rock.

"Just two people at a party together," I said out loud. That wasn't exactly what we'd be. No, she'd be a person at a party, and I'd be the puppy dog following her around all night, hoping she'd pat my head every now and then. Who the fuck was I? When had I reverted to the guy who'd done the same damn thing with Winslow?

Maybe if she and Cowboy were in attendance tonight, seeing them together would knock some sense into me. At the very minimum, I'd be reminded of the jackass I'd been when I'd asked her to marry me. As much as I didn't want to be a jackass again, I didn't know how to shake it loose.

I wanted Calla in my life so fucking bad. But she wasn't ready to move on from her dead husband. How many times did the woman have to remind me before I finally listened?

"Spider?" I heard her say from outside the door.

"Yeah?" I responded without going over to open it since I was still in my boxers.

"Rile and Kenzie should be here soon."

"Be out in a sec."

I didn't hear Calla walk away, but she didn't say anything else, either.

When I came out of the room a few minutes later, Rile and Kensington were seated in the living room with Calla.

"Sorry I wasn't here to greet you," I said, walking over to the two of them. "Don't get up," I added when Rile started to. "I'm Spider," I said to his wife, shaking her outstretched hand.

"It's nice to see you," said Rile when I shook his.

"I appreciate the invite very much." I cleared my throat, not in the mood for more small talk. "I understand you wanted to speak with Casper and me."

When I turned around, my jaw nearly dropped. Calla was dressed in a sleeveless blue gown covered in what looked like tiny crystals. The shade of blue matched her gorgeous eyes, and when she smiled at my reaction, it took my breath away. I bent down so my mouth was near her ear. "You look magnificent."

I sat beside her on the sofa, close enough so our fingers brushed when we both rested our hands on the cushion.

"Sorry for my abruptness," I said, clearing my throat.

Rile grinned. "Do you mind if we talk business for a short while, my darling?" he said, smiling at Kenzie.

"Would you like me to excuse myself?" she asked.

"Of course not, my dear."

She looked at Calla, then me. "He warned me ahead of time. I'm not sure why he's asking if I mind. Ever gallant, I suppose." She returned her gaze to him.

Under normal circumstances, witnessing their exchange wouldn't have fazed me. Now, though, I wondered if Calla would ever look at me the way Rile's wife looked at him.

"Shall we get to it, then?" he asked.

"Go ahead," Calla responded.

"As I told you when we last spoke, Fury Storm and Vex Dunning intend to offer you a partnership in the Invincibles' new team."

"I've yet to receive an offer or proposal from them."

"I asked them to hold off," said Rile.

I glanced at her in time to see Calla's brow furrow.

"The reason I intervened is because the partners of the 'first team' had a meeting yesterday, during which we voted on extending our own offers. I have not come to you with one tonight, Casper. However, when you receive it before you leave Texas, you will also receive the other. I only ask you give serious consideration to both."

She nodded but didn't speak.

Rile turned to me. "I understand you are interested in working with the Invincibles."

"I am, sir."

"It is my understanding you will be receiving offers as well. I am certain you will from the Invincibles. I have been told you should also expect one from the Unstoppables."

"The *Unstoppables*?" blurted Calla.

Rile smiled like she was. "I assure you Fury and Vex are entirely responsible for the name choice. I didn't suggest it, nor did I weigh in on it."

"Yet it sounds exactly like something you'd come up with," Calla teased.

He raised a brow. "As I was saying, Spider will be receiving offers from both entities. I'll warn you now, no one is offered a partnership prior to working directly with us for a certain amount of time. We meet once a year to confer on the subject, at which time, we compile a short list."

"Understood, and rest assured, I hoped for a contracting position, at best, sir."

Rile looked over at Calla. "You may find yourself"—he cleared his throat—"courted this evening."

"What does that mean?" she asked.

"Exactly as I said." He stood and offered his hand to his wife. "Shall we be on our way?"

I stood as he had and offered my hand to Calla. "Here I thought I was the only one who'd be courting you this evening," I whispered.

"Remember that thing I said about feeling out of my element?" she whispered.

"I do."

"Right now, I'm wishing we'd opted for Fiji."

9

Spider

"Where's this party?" I leaned over in the backseat of the SUV and asked Calla when Rile appeared to be taking us to the middle of nowhere.

"It's called the Long Branch. Hammer and his wife, Maeve, own it."

"Where Steel was a bouncer?"

"The very place."

"Fury's husband was a bouncer there too," said Rile, glancing over his shoulder.

I'd heard the story of how Tres was in the States and met Fury at a bar where the Invincibles hung out. I hit my forehead with my palm. "The Long Branch. Of course," I mumbled.

"Piecing it all together?" Calla asked, smiling.

God, she took my breath away. I covered her hand with mine. She turned it over and wove our fingers together.

Rile pulled into the spot obviously left for him by the main entrance in the otherwise packed parking lot.

"It looks as though the party has started without us," he said as he held the door and waved us inside.

"Wow," I heard Calla say. "It looks beautiful."

While I'd never been in the bar before, I agreed the space was festive. I wasn't sure what I'd expected, but not something of this size. Even from the outside, it didn't appear quite as massive.

The bar itself had to hold one hundred people, plus the high-top-table seating. To the left of it was a dining room with at least fifty tables. Directly in front of where we stood, there was a giant dance floor and a stage, where a band was playing. I wondered if the rows of strung lights above it were a permanent fixture or part of the Christmas decorations throughout the place.

As we walked over to the bar to get a drink, the band stopped playing and Rile asked if he could have everyone's attention. Rather than ordering, we walked out to the dance floor with the rest of the guests.

Decker Ashford, Keon Edgemon, and Miles Stone—known as Grinder in the intelligence community—stood beside Rile on the stage.

"Don't be shy. Come forward so I can see you," Rile said, motioning for everyone to move closer to the stage. I looked to the left and right of it, where two Christmas trees stood. Each had to be fifty feet tall, and not only were they decorated; there were gifts under them, or at least wrapped boxes made to look like gifts.

Once everyone moved toward the stage, Rile stepped up to the mic and cleared his throat. "I want to thank everyone for being here tonight. Some of you have traveled from far and wide." He looked over at Grinder, then shaded his eyes and peered at the dance floor. "Pia?"

"Here," I heard a voice say and saw a hand go up, but I didn't get a good look at the woman who'd raised it.

"I want to thank you for convincing my friend that traveling during the holidays wasn't as dreadful as he'd anticipated."

"The use of your Bombardier helped, Rile," she shouted back.

"It is always available for you and Grinder, Pia. Whenever you wish to leave your magical villa in Val d'Orcia."

"Have you been?" I leaned forward and whispered in Calla's ear. She shook her head. "We should go sometime," I added.

"Instead of Fiji?" she whispered.

"In addition to." I stared at her lips, wishing I could kiss her. Instead, I returned my gaze to the stage.

"I'm sure everyone gathered here tonight has at least one story about a Christmas spent away from family, on a mission to rescue or protect the innocent. Or being so deep undercover, it wasn't possible to even talk to your family during the holidays."

I heard many murmurs of agreement and saw several heads nod.

Rile put his hands together and looked up at the ceiling. "Whether you believe in God or not, I am thankful to Him or the universe or whatever deity kept us from sending any of you, or us"—he motioned to Deck, Edge, and Grinder—"away from our families this year."

I heard several "amens" from those in the crowd.

Decker stepped forward when Rile moved to the side, away from the mic.

"I gotta admit, I've never been big on Christmas. Until I met you." He looked down at a woman standing near the front of the stage. "I know some of you have shared my desire to avoid the hype of it, and I appreciate you being here with us tonight." He looked directly at Calla.

"Rile didn't give us much choice," said Edge, stepping up beside Decker, who laughed.

"No, he didn't." He cleared his throat, and while I wasn't standing close enough to know for certain, it appeared his eyes filled with tears.

"I'll take it from here," said Edge, grabbing Decker's shoulder, then motioning for Grinder to join him. "Rile doesn't know this, or didn't until now, but we want you all to know there's a Christmas bonus waiting in each of your bank accounts when you get home."

"And who do you think authorized all those wire transfers?" Rile shouted from a few feet to the right.

"Okay, all right, we'll admit it was his idea, in the first place," said Grinder. "However, as soon as he said it, we were all in."

"Along with that, under these two trees, you'll find gifts for each of you, along with gifts for the children who have become part of the Invincibles family over the years. I believe the count is eighteen," Edge said, looking at Decker, who nodded.

"It'll be nineteen pretty soon," a man who was ushering a woman toward the back door shouted. "Sorry to leave the party, Rile, but I believe my wife and I will be having a baby sometime tonight."

The crowd cheered, and a few of the guys followed them, presumably to see if they needed help.

"I'm sure you'll join me in wishing Rip and Pearl an easy labor and the blessed arrival of their baby girl," Rile said, stepping up to the mic when Edge and Grinder moved to the side. He raised a glass in the direction of the back door, as did everyone else who held a drink in their hand.

"As Edge said, there are gifts under the tree for each of you, and yes, the four of us are looking forward to watching the chaos of you finding them." He laughed, as did the other men on the stage, who stepped up to join him.

"Merry Christmas to all of you, and thank you for being a part of the Invincibles family," they said in unison.

"And the Unstoppables family," I heard a woman shout. Those in the crowd chuckled.

Decker looked in her direction. "I propose, next year, the Unstoppables host this shindig."

Amid more cheering, the crowd dispersed when the men left the stage and the band returned to play "Rockin' Around the Christmas Tree," clearly a crowd favorite, based on the number of couples on the dance floor.

"I'll grab some drinks," I said, motioning Calla to a high-top. She nodded and walked over to it. While I waited, I watched both men and women sifting through the gifts, either handing them to one another or making piles. Some might have considered Rile's, Decker's, Edge's, and Grinder's words trite, particularly me, who detested the holidays, but I had to admit, the atmosphere was one of a happy family, grateful to share the evening with each other.

"Do you want to look for your gift?" I asked when I set a glass of wine in front of Calla. "Or would you like me to fetch it for you?"

"You could look for mine at the same time you do yours."

I smiled. "I'm a last-minute addition, remember? I'm also not one of the family."

"Yet."

"Yet," I repeated, hoping the word meant there was still a chance Calla would want me in her life for more than her plus one at the Christmas party.

"Casper. Glad you could make it," said Decker, approaching with a woman I assumed was his wife, Mila. "Hello, Spider, and welcome," he said, shaking my hand after he'd hugged Calla.

"How are you, Mila?" she asked.

"Hanging in there, although I won't be here too long tonight." The woman rubbed her belly. "This one, along with her big brother, wears me out."

"You're having a girl! Congratulations," Calla said, hugging Decker's wife.

"Yes, congratulations," I said, shaking Deck's hand a second time.

"I'm assuming Rile spoke with you," he said.

"He did," I responded.

"Let me tell you something about this one." He pointed to Calla. "Without Casper, I don't know if my wife and I would have found our way to each other."

"There'd be no Huck," Mila added. "Or our baby girl."

"That's not true," Calla said, her cheeks turning pink.

"Of course it is." Decker nudged her after Mila excused herself. "You sure as hell put the fear of God Almighty into Adler Livingstone."

Decker explained that, as a teenager, his wife had been attacked by Livingstone's father, who'd been Mila's father's business partner and had been cheated out of millions of dollars after Judd Knight allegedly stole the patents Livingstone held for the products their company produced.

In his effort to steal the patents back, Mila's sister got caught in the crossfire and was killed.

"Are you talking about Casper's interrogation of Adler Livingstone?" Rile asked, approaching us.

"I am," Decker said. Both men looked at Calla with such admiration. I wondered if she had any idea how much they respected her. It was doubtful, given her typical humility.

"He was a pussy," she said, taking a sip of her wine.

"Sure wish I'd been able to get surveillance set up to watch that one. In the end, Casper got him to give up his father's whereabouts. Rile, Edge, and I arrived in time to see Livingstone kill Mila's dad, but Edge was able to take him out before he killed her too." Decker got choked up by the end of his recounting, like he had on stage. He cleared his throat and put his hand on Calla's shoulder. "I owe you my life, because Mila, Huck, and the new baby are my life."

"I did my job," she said, clearly uncomfortable being the center of attention.

"Hey, are you talking about how badass Casper is?" Edge asked as he approached. "You must be Spider. Welcome," he said, shaking my hand before cheek-kissing Calla. "This is my wife, Rebel."

"You saved my life too," Rebel said, nudging Calla.

She laughed. "You were zero help, by the way."

"As you probably know, we were undercover together in the ABT. Slimy *sonuvabitches*," said Edge. "Rebel was framed for the murder of one of 'em, but thanks to our friend here, we got her cleared." He put his arm around Calla, and she rested her head on his shoulder.

"You have no idea how badly I needed that mission." Her eyes met mine, and I wished I was standing close enough to put my arm around her like Edge had.

"Hey, don't leave me out," said Kenzie, joining her husband. "Casper was on my detail in Mallorca."

"Also at Christmas," said Rile. "Thankfully, there wasn't a mission this year."

"Don't jinx it," said Edge, slugging him before turning to Casper. "Rile told us to go easy on you, but when have I ever listened to him?" He laughed. "Listen, no matter whether you pick the old crew or the young one, you'll still be on our team, sweetheart. I'd just rather you be on the Invincibles' roster."

"Thanks, Edge."

The three men walked away with Rebel and Kenzie, giving us a breather.

"They aren't going to make this easy on me," she said once they were out of earshot.

I finally put my arm around her shoulders. "Are you leaning in any particular direction?"

"If the Invincibles are North and the Unstoppables are South, I'm leaning East."

"Neither?" I asked.

"I guess I'm not ready to decide."

"It hasn't been twenty-four hours, so that stands to reason."

We finished our wine and were about to look for something to eat when Cowboy and Winslow approached. I waited for the pang of jealousy that usually hit the center of my chest when I saw the two of them together, but it never struck. I was truly happy for Winslow. She'd found her match in Cowboy.

"Am I interrupting?" asked a man I'd seen photos of but, again, hadn't met—Kellen "Money" McTiernan. He was the current director of the CIA and had lent agent support to the serial killer investigation.

"She is *not* going back to the agency," said a man with a gruff voice, who had an unlit stogie in his mouth.

"Hey, Hammer," said Calla. "Do you know Spider? Hammer and his wife, Maeve, own this place."

While I'd heard of several of the Invincibles team members, I didn't recall one with the code name Hammer.

"Hammer's the attorney for the Invincibles," Casper explained.

"Was," said another woman. "Hi, I'm Fury and this is Tres," she said. "You must be Spider." She elbowed Hammer. "This ol' guy retired, and I'm now the attorney of record for both teams."

"I also heard you and Vex are heading the Unstoppables," I said.

"I am, and we're anxious to speak with you and Casper."

"But this is a party, *mi tormenta*," said Tres, nuzzling Fury's neck. I envied the man, wishing I could lean in and do the same to Calla.

"McTiernan is my brother-in-law," said Hammer. "My wife is around here somewhere. We've got plenty of staff working tonight, but she likes to check in periodically."

"At least for a dance," said Tres, winking.

"My wife insists all our employees dance at least once during their shift."

"Why?" I asked. "Not that there's anything wrong with dancing."

"If you can't have fun while you're working, you don't belong here," said Tres. "And while I'm not working, I'm ready for some fun." He took Fury's hand and led her to the dance floor.

"Shall we join them?" I said to Calla, holding my hand out to her. She hesitated long enough I thought she'd turn me down. I breathed a sigh of relief when she put her arm through mine rather than take my hand.

While the song the band was playing wasn't considered slow, I held her in my arms anyway. "Hey," I said, resting my forehead against hers. "How are you holding up?"

"I'm more accustomed to fading into the background."

"Rile warned you, you'd be wooed tonight."

"This trip down the memory lane of missions is making me uncomfortable."

"I'm sure they just want you to know how important your role was."

"As I said, I was just doing my job."

I twirled her around the floor. "You have no idea how spectacular you are, do you?"

"Because I'm not." Calla buried her head in my shoulder.

"May I cut in?" asked a guy about the size of Steel as the band started another song.

"Uh, sure."

He held out his hand. "I'm Smoke."

"Nice to meet you," I said as I turned to walk away, realizing when I was too far to turn back that I hadn't shaken his hand.

"How is Casper?" Cowboy asked when I returned to the table where we'd previously been.

My eyes scrunched. "She's fine. Why do you ask?" I'd gotten the impression from Shredder that Winslow didn't particularly care for Calla. That, coupled with the fact he'd been pretty pissed off the morning he showed up and found Calla in his bed on Canada lake, made me suspicious of his concern.

He shrugged. "Just wondering." He and Winslow left the table at the same time Buster approached.

"How's it goin', Spider?"

"Okay. Listen, Cowboy just asked me if Calla, err, Casper, was okay. There was something cryptic about it."

Buster motioned with his head at McTiernan, who was seated at a nearby table. "I heard Rile and Decker say he had something for her. Something from Beau." Buster leaned in closer. "I also heard them say they think it might've been an anniversary present. Money must not have given it to her yet."

It was as though I could feel the combined rush of cortisol and adrenaline flood my body in what could only be described as fear. *McTiernan had something for Calla from Beau.* I knew, deep in my gut, that whatever it was would make her retrace every step she'd made in my direction.

I stood, paralyzed, as I watched Smoke lead her from the dance floor to the high-top table where McTiernan waited. He pulled out a stool for her, she sat, and he handed her a small wooden box. She looked down at it, fingering the top.

"The wife of another agent who lost his life the night Beau did, found it when she was going through a box of his belongings she forgot she had. It somehow ended up there. I'm sorry, Casper," I heard him say.

She raised her head but didn't speak.

"I wish you the best of luck. Whichever team you end up on, they'll be lucky to have you."

When he stood to leave, Calla turned toward me. I stood too and took two steps over to her, but stopped when she shook her head and got up from the table. She clutched the wooden box next to her body as she bolted away in the opposite direction. I knew better than to follow.

10

Casper

I had no idea where I was running to, only that I had to run from Spider. The look in his eyes broke my heart, yet what I held in my hands was from *Beau*. My beloved husband. The love of my life. I knew whatever this box held was something I couldn't share with *anyone*, especially not Spider.

"Come with me," I heard Maeve say as she raced up and put her arm through mine. "I told my *eejit* brother this was a bloody bad idea."

I let her lead me into the office and sat in the chair she pointed to. "I'm sorry," I whispered, wiping the tears that ran down my cheeks.

"Oh, no, you're not. Kellen never should've given that to you here, now, in the middle of a fucking Christmas party."

I froze when there was a knock at the door. God, if Spider had followed me…I just…couldn't.

"No worries. I'll get rid of whoever it is. In fact, I can leave as well if you'd rather."

I set the box on the desk in front of me, afraid I'd drop it with the way my hands trembled. "Can you stay?" I asked in an equally shaky voice.

"Of course." Maeve approached the door but didn't open it. "Whoever's out there, go away."

"It's me," I heard Hammer say. "Is everything okay?"

"No!" Maeve shouted. "Everythin' is not okay. You go find my brother and kick his bloody ass all the way back to DC." She rolled her shoulders, smoothed her gown, and faced me. "Sorry. I'm sure that didn't help at all. I'm just a wee bit *angry* with Kellen, if you couldn't tell."

"It's fine," I said, smiling through my tears. I loved how straightforward and to the point Maeve always was. There was a strange comfort in it.

"That's from your dead husband," she said, motioning toward the box with her chin. "Are you gonna open it now, or would you rather I make arrangements for someone to drive us back to the ranch?"

I couldn't go to the ranch. Not yet. Eventually, Spider would show up there, if he hadn't left already, and there was no way I could face him. "I can't."

"Which, Casper?"

"I can't go to King-Alexander."

"What about the Hammered Dubliner? Would you rather go there?"

"Would you mind?"

"Not at all, considerin' this is partially my fault for not locking my brother in the cellar when he told me his harebrained idea." She pulled out her phone and placed a call. "Bring the car around the back, Hammer. I'm takin' Casper home with me." She paused. "You stay and man the place." She paused again. "Of course I can bloody drive, ya *eejit*." She shook her head and ended the call. "Men," she huffed.

No more than a couple of minutes later, her cell phone pinged. "C'mon, the car's here."

I stood and followed her.

"You sure this is what you want to do?" Maeve asked.

"I'm sure. If you're certain you don't mind."

She led me out, muttering words under her breath I couldn't decipher.

On the drive to Maeve and Hammer's ranch, I fingered the top of the box like I had earlier. Carved into it was the number five. It was rough and crude, as if the person doing it had no experience with hand carving. *Someone like Beau.*

"I don't know about you, but I could use a drink," Maeve said after leading me into the sitting room just off the foyer. She leaned down, struck a long match, and held it to the logs and kindling I had no doubt Hammer had laid before they left for tonight's party.

"That should make it cozier," she said when the fire caught. "Now. A drink?"

"Please."

"What's your fancy?"

"Whatever you've got. Straight up."

"I like the way you think, Casper."

While I looked down at the box I still held in my hands, I couldn't see it through my tears. Why now? Why hadn't someone found this right after Beau died? When I was still in the throes of the worst grief, the worst pain I'd ever known? Then, I could've handled it. Now, it brought it all back. Everything I thought I'd processed, the stages of grief I climbed my way through. It all landed back in my lap like the little wooden box did.

Maeve sat beside me on one of the loveseats and handed me a glass. She set the bottle of Irish whiskey she'd also brought with her on the table in front of us and raised her glass to me.

"To you, Casper. The bravest, most badass woman I've ever known."

I smiled through my tears. "I'm not brave," I whispered.

"Of course you are, love. You're here, aren't ya? You've faced everything life has thrown at you, and you persevered." She touched her glass to mine. "Now, drink up."

We both downed what was in the glass, and she poured us each another.

Something dawned on me. "Where's Mary?"

"Darrow is hosting a slumber party at King-Alexander. She, Tee-Tee, and Wsellie are mindin' all the wee ones. Did ya know Wellie was in town for the holidays?"

"I don't know who Wellie is," I confessed.

"Aye, well, that's a story for another time. Suffice to say he's Darrow's godfather. The man's ninety if he's a day, and yet, I bet he's got a handle on the brood they're mindin'." She motioned to the box. "Are you gonna open it?"

"Maybe another drink first."

"Aye. Just one, though." I noticed Maeve's Irish brogue became harder for me to understand the more she drank. Or maybe it was the more I drank.

I finished what was in my glass and rolled my shoulders.

"You're sure you're wantin' me to stay?" she asked.

"I don't think I'll be able to do this if you leave."

She nodded and put her hand on my arm. "Go ahead, then."

I took the lid off the box and set it on the table. Inside, there was a folded piece of paper. I opened it, and a necklace fell out into my hand. I held it up and looked at what hung from it. There were five silver rings, and inside of them, there was what looked like the blossom of a calla lily, and where the stamen would be, in its place was a heart.

"It's beautiful," Maeve gasped. "Let's put it on you."

I moved my hair, and she fastened the clasp. "Go on. Read what he wrote."

My beloved wife. This chain holds a ring for each year we've been married. Sometimes apart, but always connected. My love for you is eternal, symbolized by the heart inside you,

*my beautiful Calla lily. My heart has always
been yours, and yours has always been mine.
I'm counting the minutes until I hold you in
my arms once more. Beau*

A sob sprung from somewhere deep inside me. I handed the piece of paper to Maeve and put my head in my hands. She rubbed my back as I cried harder than I had in as long as I could remember.

"Why now?" I said when I could finally speak. "Why didn't they find this four years ago? Why now, when I think I'm finally ready to move on? *Why?"*

She held up the piece of paper. "I know not everyone believes in a higher power, but I do. Would you like to know what I think?"

I nodded and looked into her eyes.

"You just told me you thought you were finally ready to move on."

"Yes."

"With Spider?"

Tears spilled over my eyelids and down my cheeks. "Yes," I repeated.

"Tell me what you're feelin' right now? Other than profound sadness."

"I don't know."

"Guilt?"

I nodded again. "There's guilt."

"Why?"

I turned my head and stared into the fire, toying with the necklace Beau had given me. My last gift from him.

Maeve rested her hand on my arm, and I looked from the fire to her.

"I want to be with Spider," I whispered so quietly I could hardly hear myself.

Maeve nodded. "Beau isn't coming back."

"I know."

"And you have feelings for Spider. Spider? Is *that* his name?"

I smiled. "No, it's Corbin."

"*Corbin.* It's a nice strong name. Corbin what?"

"Vaughn."

"Aye, he's Welsh, then, is he?"

I looked at her with wide eyes. "He is. I mean, his ancestors are."

"He's a good man, isn't he?"

"He is. He makes me laugh and want to *do* things."

She raised a brow and poured more whiskey into our glasses. "What kinds of things?"

"Go to Fiji or spend Christmas day eating Chinese food and going to an amusement park."

Maeve's eyes bored into mine. "You've fallen in love with him, haven't you?"

"I think I have."

"Does he love you?"

While he'd never said the words, I knew in my heart he loved me. "He does."

"Where is he now?"

"I don't know."

"Then, I suggest we find him."

11

Spider

"Are you sure you want me to take you straight to the airport?" Buster asked.

"Positive," I responded, staring out the window at the black of night.

"What about your stuff?"

"Nothing I can't replace." I tugged at the end of the bow tie, and when it released, pulled it from around my neck and shoved it in my pocket. I rested my head against the seat and closed my eyes.

"Are you sure you can get a flight out tonight?"

"Positive," I repeated, even though I wasn't at all. However, even if I had to sit in the airport until tomorrow, it would be better than going back to the ranch and facing Calla. I took out my phone and opened the travel app.

There was a red-eye I could catch in two hours that stopped in Atlanta before continuing on to Palm Beach International Airport. I tapped the screen, and in mere minutes, had purchased a one-way flight in first class, and selected my seat.

"You sure you're okay?"

"Buster, if you ask me one more question, I might have to punch you in the face. Considering you're driving, that's probably not a great idea. So shut the fuck up."

The man remained silent the rest of the way to the airport. When he pulled up, I opened the door to get out and thanked him. "You're a good friend, Buster. Sorry I said I wanted to punch you."

He shrugged. "I would've said the same to you if I had the night you have."

"If anyone asks, I had a family emergency."

"You got it. See ya, Spider." He waved and I saluted.

I went inside and walked straight through security since the airport was practically empty. Conveniently, there was a bar directly across from the gate.

"What can I get you?" the bartender asked when I took a seat.

"Bourbon. Neat. And keep 'em comin'."

"You got it, sir."

I pulled a hundred-dollar bill out of my wallet and set it on the bar. Maybe I *was* destined to be an asshole just like my father. The only difference was he'd found a woman who loved him. Me? I was oh for two. Not great odds that I'd live a happy life.

I tossed back the bourbon and realized I hadn't had anything to eat since early this morning. "Is the kitchen open?"

"Lemme check." The guy walked around the bar and through a set of double doors. "Another five minutes," he said when he came back out.

"What have you got?"

"Cheeseburger isn't half bad."

"I'll take one of those."

"Fries?"

"What would a black-tie dinner be without fries?" I said, waving my hand over my tuxedo.

He laughed, shook his head, and shouted my order to the kitchen.

"Where ya headed?" he asked.

"Palm Beach."

"Damn. Wish I could join you. You golf?"

"Probably the only thing I'll be doing the next few days." I held up my glass. "Well, that and drinking."

"Sounds better than pouring beer on Christmas."

He walked away, presumably to get my food. Right now, faced with the prospect of spending the next several days with my family rather than with Calla as I'd hoped, pouring beer didn't sound that bad.

I devoured the burger and fries, turned down his offer of another drink, and walked across the way to the gate when I heard the announcement saying the flight was boarding. I sunk into my seat after grabbing a blanket and pillow from the overhead compartment. If there was a God, I prayed he'd let me sleep.

"Mr. Vaughn?" I felt a hand on my arm and opened my eyes. "We've landed, sir."

"Well, I'll be damned," I muttered, stunned I'd slept through takeoff, the entire flight, and landing. Thirty minutes from now, I'd board the next plane, and two hours after that, I'd land in Palm Beach, where I'd catch a car service to my parents' place and pray the same God who'd let me sleep on the flight would grant me six or seven straight days of it. An even twelve would be better. That way, I'd miss my family's New Year's Eve party—the one Casper was supposed to attend with me.

"What are you doing here?" I asked my mother when I walked in the front door and she greeted me. She took a step forward and kissed both my cheeks.

"Hello, Corbin. It's nice to see you too."

Only my mother insisted on calling me by my given name. Even my asshole father called me Spider.

"I thought you were leaving for Placid yesterday. Or was it the day before?"

"Dein decided he wanted to get a few rounds of golf with your father in, so he flew here instead. We'll leave Christmas Eve."

"Dein is here?" Jesus, could this get any worse? Evidently, it could, I decided when two kids came barreling at me.

"Uncle Spider!" my niece and nephew screeched. "We didn't know you'd be here! This is awesome."

"Can you take us out in the boat?" my niece Coryn asked.

"I want to go on the jet skis," shouted my nephew, Steffan.

"We can do both tomorrow, provided you allow your uncle to get some much-needed sleep."

"Why are you in your tuxedo?" my mother asked, evidently just noticing my attire. "And where is your bag?"

"I don't have one. As for why I'm dressed the way I am, that's another thing for tomorrow. Good day, everyone." I bounded up the stairs, down the hallway to the house's west wing, and into my bedroom. *My bedroom,* I thought as I closed and locked the door. I was a thirty-four-year-old man who still had a bedroom in his parents' house. And not just in one; at all of their houses. God, I was pathetic. No wonder Calla wanted nothing to do with me.

I stripped off my clothes, turned the water in the shower on, and climbed in, wishing I could think about anything other than her.

Even Winslow turning down my proposal hadn't hurt as much as watching Calla race away from me. The look in her eyes had nearly leveled me.

After brushing my teeth and washing the smell of booze and travel off my body, I shut off the water, toweled myself dry, grabbed a pair of boxers from the drawer, and climbed into bed after putting them on.

I was just about asleep when I heard a knock at the door. "Go away!" I shouted. "I told you we'd go out on the boat tomorrow."

"It's Dein. Open up, you fucking loser."

I got out of bed, stalked over to the door, and wrenched it open. "I'm a fucking loser? Guess who I met this weekend. Never mind, you'll never guess because *you've* never met her."

He pushed me out of his way, came inside, and shut the door behind him. "What are you rambling on about?" he asked as he walked over to the bedside table, picked up the remote that controlled the blinds, and opened them. I yanked it from his hand and closed them.

"As I told Mother and your children—at least two of them since that's all who live with you—Uncle Spider is not available for boat rides, jet skiing, whining, bitching, and most importantly, answering anyone's questions until tomorrow. *Now, get out!*"

"What was that remark about only two of my children living with me?"

"You know exactly what it was about." I pushed him. "I told you to get out."

The door flew open, and my father walked in. "What's all this shouting about?" he bellowed.

"I was just telling Dein how nice it was to meet his eldest daughter." I glared at my brother. "Danielle."

"What are you talking about?" my father demanded.

"As if you don't know. Give me a fucking break."

When I spun around and my eyes met my brother's, I could tell by the look on his face that my father actually didn't know.

"Dein got Susan Sweeney pregnant. If you don't remember her name, look her up. She was on the Olympic Ski Team at the same time I was. Everyone wondered why she suddenly dropped out of the competition. Come to find out—surprise, surprise—it was because my asshole brother knocked her up, then left her in the gutter. Maybe not the gutter, since he also gave her enough cash to keep the kid a secret."

"Deiniol? Is this true?" I heard my mother's voice say as she joined the three of us in my bedroom.

"Since this has *absolutely* nothing to do with me, would the three of you mind leaving so I can get some rest, please?"

My father pointed at me with his index finger. "I'll deal with *you* later. Come on, Dein. Let's hear your side of the story."

"Fuck," I seethed, walking into my closet. I grabbed a pair of shorts, a shirt, and a pair of shoes, dressing as I returned to the bedroom. Coming here had been a terrible idea. The only reason I did was because I thought they'd already left for New York. I had a place of my own, not that I was there very often. It was up the road a ways, on Jupiter Island. I'd inherited it from my grandfather, something Dein never got over. I couldn't help it if the old man liked me better, mainly because I wasn't an asshole.

I was on my way down the stairs when I realized my car was parked at the airport in Miami. "Fuck," I said out loud. By the time I drove from here to there, picked it up, then made my way back to Jupiter, it would be mid-afternoon. And while I'd slept on the plane, I needed a hell of a lot more rest. I turned around, went back to my room, and closed and locked the door—for the second time—hoping everyone would leave me the hell alone.

I must've gotten my wish, because when I opened my eyes and checked the time, I saw it was almost seven at night. There was no good reason to get up now. I rolled over and went back to sleep.

When I woke again, it was because someone was pounding on my door. Actually, they were knocking, which meant it was probably my niece. Or my mother.

I got out of bed, plucked my robe from the closet, and opened the door. "Hello, Coryn," I said, motioning for her to come inside.

"I can't go out on the boat today."

"You can't? Is that why you woke me at"—I squinted at the clock—"eight in the morning? Just to tell me that?"

"We're leaving."

"Who is?"

"Daddy, Mommy, Steffan, and me. We're going to my *other* grandparents' house for Christmas."

I'd known Dein's wife's family my entire life since their place in Lake Placid was a few doors down from ours. "I'm sure you'll be able to come over and hang out with us too."

Coryn shook her head slowly. "Grandpa said we couldn't."

"Grandpa said you couldn't come for Christmas? I don't believe you."

"Not me. Daddy."

"Ah, I see. Well, you know how Grandpa can be. He'll forget all about it by dinnertime."

"I don't think so—"

"Coryn, where are you?" we both heard her mother call for her.

The door swung open, and Eleanor marched in. "I hope you're happy," she spat at me.

"You know, you remind me of someone I ran into recently. She spoke to me in almost the exact same tone of voice. I'm sure you remember her. Susan Sweeney."

"Fuck you, Spider!" She walked over and grabbed Coryn's wrist. "Come on, we're leaving."

I stood and put my hand on her arm. "You may be angry with me or Dein or even my father, but none of this is your daughter's fault."

Eleanor released Coryn's wrist and knelt down in front of her. "I'm sorry, baby. Uncle Spider is right. Forgive me?"

Coryn nodded through tear-filled eyes and wrapped her arms around her mother's neck.

"Have a merry Christmas," she spat as she walked out of the bedroom, holding her daughter's hand rather than her wrist.

I put on the shorts and shirt I'd had on yesterday and went downstairs. If I was lucky—and I knew I wouldn't be—my brother, his family, and my parents would be gone.

"Good morning," I said, joining my mother on the terrace. Her back was to me, but when I took a step to the side, I saw she was crying.

I walked over and knelt in front of her like Eleanor had done with her daughter. "I'm sorry, Mother. I thought you knew."

Her mouth opened, then shut.

"Whatever it is, say it."

"You thought I knew? You thought I'd allow my own granddaughter to grow up without knowing her? What kind of monster do you think I am?"

"I don't think you are; I think you're married to one."

When my mother slapped my face, I stood. "I suppose I deserved that, and I'm sorry. It's just—"

She stood too, and I expected her to go inside, but she didn't. "How long have you known?"

"What day is it?"

"Don't be smart with me, Corbin."

"First of all, I'm thirty-four years old, Mother. You can't tell me not to be 'smart' with you. Second, I was serious."

"It's Christmas Eve."

"Three days."

"How did you find out?"

"I ran into Susan and her daughter at the airport. We were on the same flight, and she told me the whole story. Well, maybe not the whole story, but enough that I knew Dein was her child's father and she was paid handsomely to keep it a secret." I shook my head. "I feel like I've time-traveled to a different era. I mean, do people really still do that? Pay off someone to keep their own child a secret?"

I looked up when she did, at the car carrying my brother's family as it pulled away from the house and down the drive. "Are you really going to keep them away on Christmas? Your *grandchildren*?"

"Your father…"

"What about him?"

"He's very angry."

"So? Let him be angry. *At Dein.* Not at those two kids. They don't have a clue about what's happening."

She looked out at the water. "I have no say in this."

"Are you fucking kidding me?"

"Corbin!"

"No, this is ridiculous. I'll concede Dein is an asshole, but this happened years ago. Tell Dad to get the hell over it so you can spend Christmas with your grandkids."

"I can't."

"Can't what?" I heard my father bark from behind me.

"Tell you, you're wrong. Tell you she doesn't want Coryn and Steffan to be deprived of seeing their grandparents on Christmas. That she doesn't want to be deprived of seeing them."

"This is none of your concern. You've caused enough trouble."

"By telling the truth? Jesus. Aren't you glad you know about her? Don't you want to meet her?"

"Who is that?" my father said, looking beyond me.

I turned around and watched a car approach, stunned speechless when I saw the back door open and Calla get out.

12

Spider

"Excuse me," I heard myself say as I raced from the terrace to the driveway. "Hi. Um, what are you doing here?"

Calla held out a box. "You forgot this."

"What is it?"

"From the Invincibles."

"Oh. You didn't have to…" While I was in a state of shock, I knew that wasn't the reason she'd come. "Why are you here, Calla?"

"I needed to see you. There are things…I need to say."

There was a sharp pain in my heart. "There's no reason to tell me in person. I get it."

"I don't think you do." She looked up at the house. "Is there somewhere else we can talk?"

"God, I'm sorry. Of course we can." I motioned for her to go ahead of me. "I'll warn you. We're in the midst of some major family drama. I hope my parents don't subject you to it, but just in case."

"Over Danielle?"

I nodded. "My brother and his family left a little while ago. I confronted him about her. My parents overheard. Many angry words followed."

"I'm sorry, Spider."

"Don't be. None of this is your fault or doing. My family, well, I've made what I think of them clear."

I opened the door, and we walked inside. Thankfully, I didn't see or hear either of my parents. However, rather than leading Calla out to the terrace, I took her into the sitting room just off the foyer. "Can I get you anything? Coffee? Something to eat?"

"Can you just sit with me?"

"Of course."

When she took a seat on the sofa, I sat beside her.

"There are a lot of things I need to tell you."

And I didn't want to hear any of it. I had to, though. I had to man up. Calla came all this way. The least I could do was allow her to let me down gently. I steeled my shoulders. "Go ahead."

"What I did at the party, I'm so sorry. I was just so stunned, so overwhelmed I didn't know what to do, how to handle it."

"I understand. Receiving something from Beau had to have been quite a shock." I looked at the necklace she wore. I'd never seen it before. "Was that in the box?" I asked.

"It was."

"It's beautiful."

She touched it with her fingertips. "It's very special to me."

I nodded, unsure what to say.

"Maeve found me. She took me to the Hammered Dubliner—her and Hammer's ranch. She was with me when I opened it."

"I'm glad you weren't alone, Calla."

"I'm sorry it couldn't be you with me. I just…"

When her eyes filled with tears, I embraced her. "I understand. You don't need to explain."

She nodded and pulled away, although our arms and legs still touched.

"After I opened Beau's gift and read the message enclosed with the necklace, I came to a realization."

"That you can't be with me. I won't force you to say it. It's what I expected."

Her eyes bored into mine. "You're wrong."

"What do you mean?"

"I asked Maeve—the universe—why I had to receive Beau's gift now. Why it came when I had already mourned him and was ready to move on."

"Did the universe answer?"

"No, I don't know, maybe. Maeve did. She asked me what I was feeling. She asked if, along with profound sadness, I also felt guilt. I told her I did."

"Why, sweetheart? Over me? God, don't. I'll admit it hurts. I…care deeply for you. But I'm a big boy. At least in height. I'll get over it. Eventually."

"Is that all? Do you just care deeply for me?"

"Calla…"

"I need to know, Spider."

I closed my eyes momentarily. Would admitting my true feelings hurt more than I already did? Maybe, but she'd asked, and I'd tell her. "I love you, Calla."

"I love you, Spider…Corbin…Spider."

I smiled. "Spider works. But?"

She shook her head. "That's all. I love you."

When she moved closer, maybe to kiss me, I didn't. "What does it mean, Calla? How does it change things?"

"I want to be with you, Spider. If you'll have me."

My eyes darted back and forth between hers. "You do?"

"I do. Getting this gift from Beau meant the world to me. It always will, but there are so many things it forced me to think about. I hated that you left Texas because of me, but I think it was for the best. It made me realize that if I didn't tell you how I felt, I might lose you forever. I don't want to lose you, Spider. I love you."

"I have to admit, I feel like I'm dreaming, and when I wake up, the pain will be so unimaginable…"

"You aren't dreaming." She leaned closer and kissed me. At first, soft and gentle, almost tentative. Then full of the passion we felt for each other.

It was a dream, the best of my life, and it came to an abrupt end when I heard my father say my name.

I cupped Calla's cheek and looked over my shoulder at him.

"Pardon the interruption, but your mother and I are leaving."

I stood and held my hand out to Calla. She took it and stood too.

"Father, I'd like you to meet Calla Rey. She's someone very important to me. The *most* important person to me." I had no idea how my father would react and silently prayed he didn't do or say anything disrespectful out of the anger he felt for me.

"Winifred?" he called out for my mother, who came around the corner.

"Yes?"

"Our son has someone special he'd like us to meet." The anger I saw in his eyes moments ago was gone.

"Hello," my mother said, stepping closer.

"This is Calla Rey. As Dad said, she's someone very important to me." While I rarely referred to him that way, it felt right, now.

"Welcome, Calla. How wonderful to meet you." My mother held out her hand, and Calla dropped mine and took it.

"It's a pleasure to meet you too." She looked over at my father. "Both of you."

"Will you be joining us for Christmas?" my mother asked, looking from Calla to me.

"We will not be—"

"But we will be at your party on New Year's Eve," Calla interrupted.

I smiled when she turned to me with hopeful eyes. "Yes, we will."

"What will you do tomorrow?" my mother asked. "Forgive me. You're probably spending it with your family."

Calla reached out for me. "I am. We have a new tradition."

"The amusement park?" I asked.

She nodded. "And Chinese food."

"I see," said my mother through pursed lips. "Well, how lovely."

I laughed. "We'll talk it over, and maybe you'll see us before the party."

"We'd like that, son," said my father, who put his arm around my mother's shoulders. "I hate to cut this short, but we do have a flight to catch."

"It was wonderful to meet you," my mother repeated.

"And you."

When my parents left, I gathered Calla in my arms. "So, your family has a new tradition, does it?"

"That's right. If you're up for it."

"On one condition."

She nodded.

"We spend Christmas Eve at home."

She gasped. "My bag!"

"What about it?"

"The driver left with it."

"You brought a bag?"

"I planned to stay." She pulled out her phone. "I need to contact the car service."

"I'm sure he'll be able to come back. Maybe not today—"

"It has to be today."

Calla placed a call, and when someone answered on the other end, she explained what had happened. "He's on his way here now," she said when the call ended.

At the same time, we heard a horn beep in the driveway.

"I'll go," she said before I could, so I followed.

"At least let me carry it in for you," I said when the driver handed it to her. "Hang on," I said to him, pulling out some cash. "Have a merry Christmas," I said giving it to him without checking to see how much there was.

He looked at it with wide eyes. "Are you sure? There's—"

"I'm sure. Enjoy your holiday."

"That was very nice of you," said Calla, kissing my cheek as she passed me her bag.

I was stunned by its weight. "Whoa, what's in here?"

13

"You'll see," I told him as we walked into his parents' house. "So are we spending Christmas Eve here or—?"

"It depends on which amusement park you'd like to go to, but either way, no, we won't be staying here."

"Most of them are in Orlando."

"Then, if you don't mind, we'll stay at my place. It isn't a whole lot closer than here, but definitely closer than Miami would be. Although I will have to go down there eventually to get my car."

"We could do that today if you'd like."

"Nah, my parents have others they keep here. I'll use one of theirs."

"God, they really are rich," I said when he led me into the garage. "How many does this hold?"

Spider shrugged. "Not sure. Maybe twenty." He pointed down the row. "Any you'd prefer over another?"

I laughed. "All of them look pretty nice."

He walked over to a Range Rover, opened the passenger door for me, and set my bag in the backseat. "This is the most comfortable," he said, as if he needed to qualify his choice.

"It's only been eight days since I was last here," he said, turning into the drive. "It feels like a lifetime ago."

I had to agree. One lifetime had ended and another began in a little over a week.

"Wow!" I exclaimed as a yellow house with a blue roof came into view. "It's…huge."

"It belonged to my grandparents. They left it to me. Something Dein will never forgive me for."

"You're nicer than he is."

He laughed. "Exactly. Oh, and compared to your place, this is slightly dated."

Based on the little I could see when we pulled up, it looked immaculate, dated or not.

"Um, Rather than go in through the garage, I'll take you in the front door. Better views." He pulled up and parked. "While this fronts Indian River, there's a pathway out to the beach, there."

"Wow," I repeated, taking in the view as he punched in a code, opening the front door. Spider motioned me inside.

"One more warning. The kitchen is nice, although not as spectacular as yours."

I rolled my eyes. "I don't believe you." I walked over to the wall of windows that looked out at the river. "Is that your boat?" I pointed to the end of the dock.

"It is. Not that I use it much. It's a nice day. Would you like to take it out later?"

"I'd love to."

"Your wish is my command." He set my bag on the floor, near the staircase, walked over, and put his arms around me. "You being here is the best gift I've ever received in my life, Calla."

"I feel the same way about you. And before you question me, I truly do, Spider. I never dreamed I'd have a second chance at love." My eyes filled with tears. "I'm so grateful."

Spider put his hands on each side of my face, leaned in, and kissed me. "I love you. I can't tell you how badly I've wanted to say those words to you."

"I wasn't ready to hear them, but now, I want to hear them again and again and again."

"I love you." He kissed my nose. "I love you." Then my right cheek. "I love you," he repeated each time he kissed a different part of my body. "I want you so much, but I don't want to rush this."

"We have the rest of our lives, Spider." I felt my cheeks heat, hoping he wanted the same thing I did.

There was a glint in his eyes. "A lifetime, Calla. And you're right. Rather than lift you into my arms and carry you up the stairs and into my bedroom, maybe we should hold off. Spend the day tormenting each other a little."

As much as I wanted to make love right now, where we stood, I also wanted to hold off and take some time to get used to the fact that we'd finally confessed our feelings.

He'd used the right word when he said we'd spend the day tormenting each other. Or maybe torture would have been more appropriate.

We took a boat ride down the river and back, where he pointed out different landmarks, places he'd hung out and played when he was growing up and visited his grandparents.

"Hungry?" he asked.

I was starving, but not for food. I wanted Spider, naked and under me, so I could be the one to control our pleasure.

He held out his hand and pulled me over to where he stood, his hands on the wheel—or helm, as he'd called it—of what he'd told me was a vintage motor cruiser he'd slowly restored in the last five years. The boat had belonged to his grandfather and was part of his inheritance. He'd bought it in the forties, but in the final years of his life, hadn't been able to keep it up the way he had in years past.

"I wish I would've known. Dein and I could've worked on it for him. Every time I asked about it, he told me it was in storage."

While he talked, he switched positions with me so I was the one with my hands on the helm, then he pointed to something in the distance. "Make sure the bow of the boat is headed toward it."

"Where are you going?"

"Nowhere. I'll be right here." He sunk to his knees and turned me so I was at a slight angle to the helm and put his hands on my hips. "I have to see you, Calla." He nuzzled his face between my legs. "Will you let me?"

"As long as you don't blame me if we crash." My voice was heavy, husky, and full of want.

"You're going to have to concentrate on the bow so we don't."

"I can't, Spider," I whined at the same time he pulled my shorts and panties down to my ankles and I stepped out of them.

"You can, baby. Let me have a taste of you."

I clutched the helm with both hands, hanging on more than steering while Spider licked and laved between my folds, his fingers alternating between my clit and thrusting inside me.

I screamed his name as an orgasm shot from the tip of my head to my toes, leaving me shuddering and clinging to the helm with one hand and his shoulder with the other.

"Give me another one, baby. Come on."

Spider's fingers curled inside me, pressing against my G-spot while his tongue flicked my clit. What felt like seconds after I'd come down from the first climax, another almost brought me to my knees.

Spider wiped his mouth with the back of his hand and tugged my shorts and panties over my butt. If his arms hadn't gone around me to hold me, I would've melted into a puddle at his feet. I reached for the obvious bulge in his shorts when he stood, but Spider grabbed my wrist.

"Hey, no fair. If you get to touch—and lick—so do I."

He smiled. "That would be if you're making the rules, sweetheart, but you aren't."

"Says who?" I put one hand on my hip when Spider put one of his on the helm.

"I do."

"When do I get to make them?"

"Stroke of midnight."

"What do we do? Take turns?" I asked.

Spider grinned. "I like that idea, and by the looks of it, so do you." He reached out and tweaked my nipple.

I rested one hand on his shoulder, so tempted to do the same to him, but tomorrow, I'd make him pay.

"I gotta know what you're thinking, sweetheart."

"Tomorrow, I'm in charge, and we're going to find every single hidden-away place we can in that amusement park, and with each one we locate, I'll do whatever I want to your body."

"Challenge accepted." He pulled me into him and pressed his tongue against the seam of my lips. I could taste myself as he swirled his tongue with mine.

"Can we go back to the house now?" I pleaded.

"Not quite yet. We were hungry, remember?"

"I'm not hungry."

"Sure, you are." He winked. "Remember, I'm in charge until midnight."

Spider pulled the boat up to a dock, where two teenage guys waited to tie it off.

"Hey, Spider," one of them said.

"Hey, take care of my girl, you understand?"

"Always." The one who'd said Spider's name was looking at his boat like it was a Ferrari. On the other hand, maybe the boat was worth more than a car.

I expected Spider to lead me inside, but he stood on the dock, seemingly lost in thought.

"Everything okay?" I asked.

"What?" He looked like he'd just come out of a fog.

"I asked if everything was okay."

"Yeah, it's great. I just thought of something I need to do."

"Do you want to leave?

"No way. I'm starving, and I know you are too, even though you won't admit it."

Once inside the restaurant and I detected the heavenly aroma of steak cooked on a grill, my mouth watered.

"Told you," said Spider, nudging me. "Best steaks this side of Texas."

I punched his arm. "You haven't spent enough time in Texas to know." As soon as I spoke the words, I regretted them. He'd left after being there less than twenty-four hours, because of me. Because I'd hurt him. I turned away but felt his arm snake around my waist.

"Don't go there, Calla. It's Christmas Eve, and we're together. That's all that matters."

"But—"

He shut me up with a kiss, then led me to our table.

"Good to see you, Spider," said the older gentleman with a heavy Welsh accent who handed us our menus.

"Calla, I'd like you to meet one of my grandfather's closest friends, Alfred Miller. Alfred, meet Calla, the love of my life."

I stared at Spider wide-eyed, then remembered he'd just introduced me to someone. "Um, hi, Mr. Miller. It's so nice to meet you."

"The pleasure is all mine, my dear, and please call me Alfred." The man winked and left the table. Spider pulled the chair by the window out for me, then took the seat beside me rather than across.

"You are, you know."

"Spider, I…"

"You don't have to say it back to me. You've already said the three words I didn't think I'd ever hear. Those are the ones that matter."

"I do love you."

"I know, and nothing means more to me." He leaned in closer and put his arm around me. "I know you're never going to forget Beau, and I know I'll never take his place. I haven't had a great love in my life until you. If it makes you uncomfortable for me to do what I did, say what I said, to Alfred. I won't do it again."

I shook my head and brought my hand to his face. "You are such a gift to me, to my life."

"Does that mean I don't have to get you anything for Christmas?"

I kissed his cheek and whispered in his ear, "You don't, but wait until you see what I have for you."

14

Spider

I didn't want to leave Calla alone at the table, but I needed to talk to Alfred. He was the only one I'd trust to take care of what I wanted to have done. Finally, when she excused herself to the ladies' room, I waved him over. I grabbed a pen and wrote something on the back of the napkin. "For the cruiser," I said, pressing it into his hand.

"*Finally.* When?"

"As soon as you can make it happen."

"I have been known to be a miracle worker," he said, reading what I'd written.

"I'll pay whatever it takes."

"I'll have it taken care of."

"You'll call me?"

Before he could answer, Calla returned to the table.

"Andrew said there's something amiss with your gas line. He's looking at it now, but I don't know how much longer it'll take. Do you want to pick her up in the morning?" Alfred asked.

"We have a full day tomorrow. In case you've forgotten, it's Christmas." I winked. "Just let me know when it's ready, and I'll make arrangements to come and get it."

Alfred nodded and left the table.

"I don't want to stick my nose in where it doesn't belong, but should you tell him you don't expect Andrew, whoever he is, to work on Christmas Eve?" Calla asked.

"I got the message across. Now, dessert or home?"

"Dessert at home"

"I like the way you think, sweetheart."

We studied the menu and chose the chocolate torte with raspberry sauce and crème brûlée. When he delivered the boxes to our table, Alfred informed us there was a car waiting outside to take us to my house.

We rode in silence, the air thick between us. Calla's hand on my thigh slowly, painfully, moved closer to the place my rigid cock would have peeked out from the hem of my shorts if it weren't for my boxer briefs.

The way she squeezed her thighs together made it obvious she suffered from the same agonizing desire I did. Yet, as much as I wanted her, needed her, I appreciated that we'd waited what felt like an eternity, but was only a few days. Had we allowed desire to fuel our intimacy the night we'd spent at Raspoutine, what would happen between us tonight would not feel as right. Now that we'd confessed our love to each other, we could express the emotion with our bodies as much as our words.

When the driver pulled up to the front door of the house, Calla exited the vehicle before I had time to come around and get her door. We met at the top of the steps, and I punched in the code I'd reprogrammed the day I returned from Canada Lake—22552.

She wasn't looking when we'd arrived earlier, but this time, she noticed. Her eyes met mine, and we stood immobile, not crossing the threshold as eagerly as we'd raced to the door.

"Spider—"

I leaned forward and kissed her. Our tongues danced the same way our bodies had at the Christmas party. I held her nape with one hand and covered her breast with the other, pinching her hardened nipple between two fingers. "Inside. Now, Calla."

If she hadn't turned from my arms and done as I demanded, I would've stripped her naked and taken her on the landing; that was how much I wanted her.

Once inside, I led her over to the staircase, lifted her in my arms, and carried her up to the hallway leading to my bedroom. Tomorrow or the day after that or the next one, we'd make love all over my house, in every room, on the stairs, out by the pool—everywhere. Tonight, I needed her in my bed, where I'd spent sleepless nights fantasizing about what was about to become reality.

I set her on the end of the bed and pulled the T-shirt she wore over her head, then reached around and unclasped her bra. "I need you naked, baby." She rested on the bed, and I pulled her shorts and panties over her ass and down her legs. There'd be time for the slow tease of stripping each other bare later. Now, I needed her fast and hard. No preamble.

She scooted up the bed so her head rested on the pillows and opened her legs. I put both hands on the crease between her legs and her pussy and spread her folds with my thumbs. As much as I wanted to taste her, feel her flood my tongue with her essence, I couldn't wait.

"Please, Spider," she said, her eyes boring into mine.

"Tell me what you want, Calla. Do you want my mouth?"

She shook her head. "I need you inside me."

"This?" I winked and ground my erection against her liquid heat. "You have to wait a little bit longer."

"Why?" she whined.

"Condom, sweetheart."

Her hand clasped my wrist. "I haven't been with a man since…"

I was grateful she didn't say his name. Her dead husband and any memories of him didn't belong in bed with us.

"I haven't been with another woman since before we met, and once we had, I knew I'd wait for you and you alone, no matter how long it took."

"No condom, Spider. I want to feel you. Nothing between us ever again."

I settled between her legs and eased my cock into her. She was burning hot, drenched, and so tight my eyes rolled back in my head.

"Give me more," she demanded.

"At midnight, you can take over, baby. Right now, I'm in charge." If I didn't take this slow, I wouldn't last. I angled my hips, giving her what she'd asked for. When our eyes met and Calla clenched around me, it was like a bolt of lightning struck me. What I felt for this woman was more than words could convey. I loved her. I would for the rest of my life. I'd honor, protect, and vow to make her smile, make her life, make her happy every day we were blessed to spend together.

I thrust deeper, sliding my hands under her ass, increasing my rhythm until her cheeks flushed as her fingernails dug into my arms where her hands rested.

"Come with me," she pleaded.

I exploded into her at the same time her back arched and she cried out, "Spider."

Hearing *my* name on her lips, knowing she was mine now, nearly brought me to tears. I eased from her body, rolled to her side, and gathered her in my arms.

"Saying I love you feels so inadequate."

She smiled and cupped my cheek with her soft hand. "You just showed me what words can't express."

I covered her hand with mine and brought her palm to my lips. "This is the happiest day of my life, and I know that sounds stupid and immature and cheesy, but it's true."

She inhaled as if she was about to speak, but I covered her lips with my fingertips.

"There's something I need to say. Do. Say and do. I was going to wait until tomorrow, but I can't."

I released her from my arms, reached to the bed-side table, and turned the light on. Calla walked over to where I'd set her bag earlier.

I watched as she pulled out two boxes wrapped with Christmas paper, then picked up the one she'd brought with her from Texas that was sitting on the dresser.

When Calla knelt on the bed, facing me, I wrapped my arm around her, nestling her nakedness closer to me. I sat up when she handed me the biggest of the three boxes. "This is what made your bag so heavy."

She smiled and watched as I removed the lid and peeled away the layers of tissue paper. I reached in and pulled out a piece of what could only be lead crystal, given its weight. It was made of red glass, and its many facets were cut into the shape of a heart.

I looked into Calla's eyes. "There was a time I believed my heart would belong to Beau for all eter-nity. Today, I'm giving it to you." She put her hand on mine and turned the piece of glass over. Etched into the bottom were the words "Calla's Heart."

I brought it to my lips, kissed the words, then kissed her. No gift had ever meant more other than her telling me she loved me.

"I will treasure, protect, and honor this and you every day for the rest of my life."

"And I'll do the same for you." She looked down at the two other packages. "Rile came to the Hammered Dubliner the morning after the party and asked to see me. I came downstairs and found him waiting in the foyer, and he had these two packages with him. He made me promise I would get yours to you."

"Do you want to do that now?" I asked, setting the glass heart on the bedside table.

"I feel like we're supposed to."

"Okay. Count of three?"

She rolled her eyes, and I watched as she painstakingly unwrapped and folded the paper I'd torn open. The boxes underneath were the same size and shape.

We lifted the lids at the same time. I glanced over and saw hers was a frame like mine was. I turned it over, and behind the glass was a photo of Calla. Near the bottom, a handwritten note read, "The cost of not following your heart is spending your life wishing you had."

Calla turned her frame over. Under the glass was a photo of me, one I'd never seen before. At the bottom, the same note was written.

"Rile's doing?" I asked.

She laughed. "Definitely. The man has never been known for subtlety."

"Maybe we should send him a selfie."

"In bed? Both of us naked?"

"You said he wasn't known for subtlety." I took the frame from her hands. "I have a better idea. Get under the covers with me. Wait. Where's your phone?"

"You aren't really suggesting we send him a photo?"

"Trust me."

Calla climbed off the bed and picked up her cell from where it sat on the dresser.

"This way, if you decide you don't want to send it, you don't have to."

She raised a brow but handed it to me, then crawled into bed. I snuggled her close, pulled the blanket up to both our chins, and cupped her cheek, turning her face to mine. With my other hand, I held up the phone and took a close-up shot of us kissing.

"How'd it turn out?" I asked, showing her the screen before I looked at it.

"It's perfect." She took the phone from my hand and turned it so I could see it.

It was a simple kiss, yet it conveyed love. Pure, simple, and true. "That's my favorite photo of us."

Calla kissed my cheek. "That's the only photo of us."

"Even after we have hundreds, that one will still be my favorite."

"Merry Christmas, my love," I said sometime after midnight. "Your turn to make the rules."

"Mmm, Merry Christmas," she said, pulling the blanket out of her way.

What she did next ensured I'd let her make the rules whenever she wanted to, every day, for the rest of our lives.

"While the idea of going to an amusement park today sounds fun, I think I'd be happier just staying here. And by here, I mean right here—in bed," Calla said when we woke early the next morning after making love most of the night.

"You're the boss, sweetheart, at least until midnight. I do have one request, though."

Her back had been to mine, but she rolled over. "A Christmas wish?"

"Something like that. Although, I'm pretty sure you've made every wish I've ever had come true already."

Her cheeks turned pink. "You've made mine come true too, Spider. Even the wishes I didn't realize I had."

"It means leaving the bed. And the house."

"I suppose I could live with that as long as we aren't driving three hours north, then back again."

This is much closer. I'd like to check on the boat today. Maybe sometime this afternoon."

"Do you think anyone will be at the marina today?" Calla asked.

"I know they will. For years, Alfred has hosted a Christmas dinner for everyone in Jupiter who'd other-wise spend it alone."

"How sweet. I love that. Do you think he could use some help?"

"I hadn't thought of that, but maybe." I had an entirely different reason for wanting to go to the marina, and since we weren't going to Orlando today, it would work out perfectly.

I went downstairs to make us coffee and called Alfred. "I know I said we wouldn't be around today—"

"Everything is ready. We were able to appease Poseidon with your champagne last night. The lads have been busy as Santa's elves this morning, preparing the rest."

"Thank you, Alfred. I can't tell you how much I appreciate this."

"I chided you enough for waiting. Now, I know why you did."

I ended the call seconds before Calla joined me in the kitchen.

"Alfred said she's ready."

"Great. Did you ask him if he needed help?"

"He would've said no even if he did. Better to show up and volunteer."

"What time is dinner served?" she asked.

"I think it's an all-day kind of thing."

Calla put her arms around my waist. "You were fibbing about your kitchen. I think it's nicer than mine."

"Yeah?"

"It's definitely bigger. I'm thinking I'd like to give it a whirl. See if it lives up to my expectations."

"If you're suggesting breakfast—especially if pancakes are involved—I'm all in. Wait. I don't have buttermilk."

"Do you have butter?"

I nodded.

"Cream?"

I opened the fridge. "Will regular milk work?"

She came up behind me and put her arms around my waist. "Do you have any idea how many times I wanted to do this when we were in the Adirondacks?"

I turned in her arms. "Make breakfast?"

"This." Calla put her hands on my bare chest. "And this." She kissed the hollow of my neck, then up the side of it and across my cheek to my lips.

I lifted her in my arms and moved her far enough away that I could close the refrigerator door, then put my hands on either side of her face.

"You wanted to kiss me?" I asked.

She smiled and nodded. "Especially when I walked into the kitchen and found you shirtless."

"Do you have any idea how hard it was for me to, uh, hide my attraction to you?"

She chuckled. "I'd say I know exactly how *hard* it was."

"I don't know whether to be mortified or flattered. I also don't understand why you never said anything."

"Be flattered, and the timing wasn't right. Now, it is."

We didn't arrive at the marina until mid-afternoon. By then, the restaurant and bar were both packed. Alfred, dressed in a Santa suit, came around to greet us. "Happy Christmas!" he shouted over the din of the crowd.

"Merry Christmas, my friend," I said, shaking his hand after he and Calla embraced.

"Come with me." He motioned for us to follow him to the docks on the opposite side of where I'd left the boat the night before.

"He seems pretty busy. Are you sure you want to do this now?" Calla whispered once we were outside.

"*I'm* certain," Alfred said over his shoulder, winking.

"Calla, this is Andrew," I said when he met us near the boat's bow. "Thanks for getting her ready."

"Aye, 'twas a labor of love."

"Andrew is Alfred's son," I explained in response to Calla's raised brow, even though I knew that wasn't what she was questioning.

"Fixing your gas line was a labor of love?" she whispered.

"That wasn't exactly what they were doing."

"Wait, what were—"

Before she could ask, people we'd seen in the restaurant and at the bar began filing down onto the docks. Two women stepped forward, each carrying a bottle of champagne—Veuve Clicquot, of course.

"For Poseidon," the first one said, handing me her bottle.

"And for you." The second woman winked and handed a bottle wrapped in mesh to Calla.

"What's going on?" she whispered.

"You'll see."

Andrew let out a loud whistle, and the crowd went silent.

Alfred cleared his throat and unfurled a scroll. "Oh, mighty rulers of the winds, through whose power our frail vessels traverse the wild and faceless deep, we implore you to grant this worthy vessel the benefits and pleasures of your bounty."

I opened the bottle I held and poured some into the two flutes Andrew held out to me.

While Alfred read on, I poured the rest of what was in the bottle in the sea, stopping to turn my body ninety degrees until I'd completed a full circle.

"Boreas, Zephyrus, Eurus, and Notus, exalted rulers of the winds, grant us permission to use your mighty powers in the pursuit of our lawful endeavors, ever sparing us the overwhelming scourge of your scalding breath."

When he finished, I walked over to Calla. "When you christen a boat with a new name, tradition states you must first appease Poseidon and the gods of the wind. When I refinished her, Alfred asked me what I'd rename her. I knew the answer then, but I was afraid to say it out loud. Afraid you'd never love me the way I love you." I kissed her and took the bottle from her hand. "Come with me."

I led her to the boat's transom and positioned her in front of me on the dock. Andrew was on board, and when my eyes met his and I nodded, he grabbed the tarp and lifted it.

I leaned forward and kissed the cheek of the woman whose name graced the stern.

"Time for the christening," bellowed Alfred, raising a glass as the crowd cheered and raised the ones they held.

We walked to the bow. "Put your hands on mine," I said, motioning to where I gripped the bottle.

"I christen thee 'For the love of Calla.'" As the bottle smashed against the boat's bow, I leaned into the woman next to me. "Merry Christmas, my love."

Epilogue

Spider

"What have you decided?" I asked, plucking two glasses of champagne from the trays the staff at my parents' New Year's Eve party passed around.

"Why do I have to be the one to decide?"

"Because today is your day to make the rules."

Calla looked at the clock on the mantle. "In fifteen minutes, it will be your turn."

"We could flip a coin."

"No. I've decided." She bit her bottom lip.

"Do you want me to guess?"

Calla smiled. "Sure."

"The Unstoppables."

"How did you know?"

"I've known all along," I said, leaning forward to kiss her like I had hundreds of times since Christmas Eve. I looked up at the clock, making sure I had enough time to respond. "Because we don't have to fit into a mold that's already been cast. This team will be as much ours as it is Fury's and Vex's."

"I'm glad they offered you a partnership too."

"Even if they hadn't, I knew it's where you'd want to be." I glanced at the time again.

"Is it getting close to midnight? You keep looking at the clock."

"I want to show you something." I took her hand and walked over to the French doors that led to the heated terrace. As we crossed the threshold, I pressed the button on the remote control that had been in the left pocket of my tuxedo all night.

"It's so beautiful," Calla gasped.

I put my arms around her and spun us both in a circle, letting the warmth of a thousand red and white twinkling overhead lights bathe us in their glow. All around us were decorated Christmas trees of various sizes, but the largest stood in the center of the space with a single chair beside it.

Inside, the revelers began the countdown. I raised my glass and stared into Calla's eyes. "I love you."

"I love you," she said.

At the stroke of midnight, we kissed, then I led her over to the chair by the tree. When she sat, I got down on one bended knee, reached into my jacket's right pocket, and pulled out the box that had also been there since the beginning of the night.

"Will you marry me, Calla?" I said, holding the ring that had been inside out to her.

"Yes, I'll marry you."

I slid the ring on her finger, and as I kissed her, I pulled my phone out of my back pocket. I held it up and snapped a picture.

"Let me see," she said, giggling.

I turned the phone around before looking at the screen. "How'd it turn out?"

"It's perfect," she beamed. "*This* is my favorite photo of the two of us."

"We never sent the other one to Rile."

Calla took the phone, tapped the screen, and I heard the swoosh of the message being sent right before I heard the whiz of the first of the fireworks, shooting into the sky above us.

"Happy New Year, soon-to-be Mrs. Vaughn."

"Happy New Year, my soon-to-be husband."

About the Author

USA Today and Amazon Top 15 Bestselling Author Heather Slade writes shamelessly sexy, edge-of-your seat romantic suspense.

She gave herself the gift of writing a book for her own birthday one year. Forty-plus books later (and counting), she's having the time of her life.

The women Slade writes are self-confident, strong, with wills of their own, and hearts as big as the Colorado sky. The men are sublimely sexy, seductive alphas who rise to the challenge of capturing the sweet soul of a woman whose heart they'll hold in the palm of their hand forever. Add in a couple of neck-snapping twists and turns, a page-turning mystery, and a swoon-worthy HEA, and you'll be hol ding one of her books in your hands.

She loves to hear from my readers. You can contact her at heather@heatherslade.com

To keep up with her latest news and releases, please visit her website at www.heatherslade.com to sign up for her newsletter.

MORE FROM AUTHOR HEATHER SLADE

BUTLER RANCH
Kade's Worth
Brodie's Promise
Maddox's Truce
Naughton's Secret
Mercer's Vow
Kade's Return
Butler Ranch Christmas

WICKED WINEMAKERS
FIRST LABEL
Brix's Bid
Ridge's Release
Press' Passion
Zin's Sins
Tryst's Temptation

WICKED WINEMAKERS
SECOND LABEL
Beau's Beloved
Coming Soon:
Cru's Crush
Bones' Bliss
Snapper's Seduction
Kick's Kiss

ROARING FORK RANCH
Coming Soon:
Roaring Fork Wrangler
Roaring Fork Roughstock
Roaring Fork Rockstar
Roaring Fork Rooker
Roaring Fork Bridger

THE ROYAL AGENTS
OF MI6
Make Me Shiver
Drive Me Wilder
Feel My Pinch
Chase My Shadow
Find My Angel

K19 SECURITY
SOLUTIONS TEAM ONE
Razor's Edge
Gunner's Redemption
Mistletoe's Magic
Mantis' Desire
Dutch's Salvation

K19 SECURITY
SOLUTIONS TEAM TWO
Striker's Choice
Monk's Fire
Halo's Oath
Tackle's Honor
Onyx's Awakening

K19 SHADOW OPERATIONS
TEAM ONE
Code Name: Ranger
Code Name: Diesel
Code Name: Wasp
Code Name: Cowboy
Code Name: Mayhem

K19 ALLIED INTELLIGENCE
TEAM ONE
Code Name: Ares
Code Name: Cayman
Code Name: Poseidon
Code Name: Zeppelin
Code Name: Magnet

K19 ALLIED INTELLIGENCE
TEAM TWO
Coming Soon:
Code Name: Puck
Code Name: Michelangelo
Code Name: Typhon
Code Name: Hornet
Code Name: Reaper

PROTECTORS
UNDERCOVER
Undercover Agent
Undercover Emissary
Coming Soon:
Undercover Savior
Undercover Infidel
Undercover Assassin

THE INVINCIBLES
TEAM ONE
Decked
Edged
Grinded
Riled
Smoked

THE INVINCIBLES
TEAM TWO
Bucked
Irished
Sainted
Hammered
Ripped

THE UNSTOPPABLES
TEAM ONE
Furied
Merried

COWBOYS OF
CRESTED BUTTE
A Cowboy Falls
A Cowboy's Dance
A Cowboy's Kiss
A Cowboy Stays
A Cowboy Wins